DARK INTENT

DARK INTENT

RAE FOLEY

G.K. Hall & Co. • Chivers Press
Thorndike, Maine USA   Bath, Avon, England

This Large Print edition is published by G.K. Hall & Co., USA and by Chivers Press England.

Published in 1996 in the U.S. by arrangement with Golden West Literary Agency.

Published in 1996 in the U.K. by arrangement with the author's estate and Golden West Literary Agency.

U.S. Hardcover 0-7838-1653-7 (Romance Collection Edition)
U.K. Hardcover 0-7451-4771-2 (Chivers Large Print)

G.K. Hall Large Print Romance Collection.

The text of this Large Print edition is unabridged.
Other aspects of the book may vary from the original edition.

Set in 16 pt. News Plantin by Minnie B. Raven.

Printed in the United States on permanent paper.

British Library Cataloguing in Publication Data available

Library of Congress Cataloging in Publication Data

Foley, Rae, 1900–
    Dark intent / Rae Foley.
        p.   cm.
    ISBN 0-7838-1653-7 (lg. print : hc)
    1. Large type books.   I. Title.
[PS3511.O186D37   1996]
813'.54—dc20   95-53788

FOR NANNINE JOSEPH
GUIDE, PHILOSOPHER AND FRIEND

ONE

Roger Brindle was dead. From New York to California people read the story with the same unbelief, the same sense of loss. Unbelief that anyone so brimming with life could die. A sense of loss because Roger had established a curiously personal relationship with the readers of his syndicated column *The Way I Heard It.*

When they opened their papers that Monday evening and turned to Roger's daily chatter about his friends and neighbors, they found a black-bordered portrait and under it the words, "Died in his sleep," and to most of them it seemed that something warm and vital had gone out of their lives.

Radio commentators gave brisk accounts, hastily culled from the morgue, of his phenomenal success as a writer for big-city newspapers about small-town people and their affairs. On a memorial program a half-dozen speakers paid tribute to him as a human being and told I-Knew-Him-When stories of the big, modest, kindly man who had made the people of a nation his neighbors. Unlike most success stories, those about Roger Brindle were records of friendships.

While the slow cortege moved along the green at Stoweville and out of the village to the cemetery, a city reporter in search of local color joined a group of men who stood outside the hardware store, watching.

"Any of you know Brindle?"

"We all knew him. I saw him only a week ago in Paul's Barbershop. He looked kinda flushed but you wouldn't have thought he was a sick man. He called me by name."

"No side to him. He's always been the same. You'd see him coming along, towering above everyone on the street —"

"How tall was he?"

"Maybe six-four. Homely as sin but you couldn't ask for a nicer expression."

"No one to take his place."

"Not by a long shot. Funny how, even if you didn't know him well, you felt like he was a friend of yours."

"Hey! See that?"

"What?"

"Woman in the green car — no, right in front of you —"

"What about her?"

"I guess she was before your time. Roger Brindle's first wife, that's all. Only time she's been here since the divorce. Ten years if it's a day. She's changed some, a bit heavier and a little gray in her hair. But there's no doubt — that's Jane Brindle."

"Kind of queer for both wives to be here, isn't it?"

"I never could figure out why Jane left him."

"Neither could anyone else. At least, his second marriage worked out."

"Poor girl. But Carol is good looking and only thirty. Fifteen years younger than Roger. She'll marry again. It's the people he helped who are more to be pitied. Take the Kibbees. Roger and Albert Kibbee have been friends since they were kids. Roger supported Albert most of his life. And Albert's wife. Even put their son through college."

"I never knew the Kibbees had a boy."

"That was Roger for you. Not a word about what he was doing for people. The way he wrote them up in his column, you'd think the Kibbees and the rest of them were the ones who did things for him. That's Mrs. Kibbee in the sedan. Must be her son with her. He sure has been kept under wraps since he came here."

"Why doesn't Kibbee go out and get himself a job?"

"He's a minister of one of those obscure sects. He'd get a job or a call or whatever it is, and a year later he'd lose his church. Roger always said Albert had too big a spirit to be confined to any dogma. Don't know myself. I thought he was an unimpressive little runt but don't let my wife hear that. Roger said he was a saint, so he's a saint."

"More than anyone could say about Joe Hattery."

"That's Roger again. Taking in an ex-convict and giving him a second chance. He let the

Hatterys have one of those little cottages and kept Joe working around the place so's to have an eye on him and see he went straight. He made Mrs. Hattery his secretary. Way he wrote about her in his column, you'd think he was the fortunate one and his secretary did half his work."

"I'll be damned! This funeral is bringing out even the ghosts. Believe it or not, that's Shandy Stowe in the convertible."

"Stowe! I thought he'd died or moved away."

"Nope. The war messed him up some and he sold his house to Brindle and moved into a little cottage. Like a hermit."

"First Stowe since there was a Stoweville not to take an interest in the town. What does he do with all his money?"

"Pity Roger Brindle didn't have part of it. I wonder what his wife will do now."

ii

That was what Carol Brindle was wondering. She had returned from the funeral, shutting the door firmly against everyone who wanted to see her, except for Max Griswold who had been Roger's attorney and general man of business. He insisted on talking to her without delay.

"There is almost no money," he told her bluntly. "I don't understand it. Roger was —" he went on with caution — "sometimes he seemed a little odd these past months. Worried about something."

"Odd in what way?"

Something in Carol's voice, a startled note, made the lawyer give her a speculative glance. "He got fits of depression. Just a month ago, he told me he never managed to do things right, no matter how he tried. Of course, he always expected the impossible of himself. But still — and he said a queer thing. He said, 'Max, it's ridiculous for me to make a will. As though I could leave anything.' Didn't sound to me as though he meant property but as though he thought he would vanish without leaving a trace." Griswold's hands made a helpless gesture. "I can't explain it. As though — Roger had never been. Morbid, anyhow."

"No!" Carol's voice did not lose its softness but there was no mistaking her fierce rejection of his implication. "No, Max! He wasn't like that at all. Roger was happy, the happiest man I ever knew."

"Well," Griswold suggested, "perhaps he had a subconscious awareness that he was seriously ill. Could be something like that. Queer, I never knew he had a heart condition."

"He just — died in his sleep," Carol said.

"Well, my dear girl," Griswold said more briskly, "we'll have to figure out something for you. The blunt truth, and there's no way of softening it, is that Roger didn't leave more than five thousand dollars. Unless you sell the house —"

"I'll never sell the house! It was Roger's wedding present to me; I love this place. The first time I saw it I wanted to live here."

"But what are you going to do?" he expostulated. "I know Roger was too generous for his own good but he should have thought of you."

Roger's young widow turned on the old man with a fierceness that startled him.

"He did think of me! I was first with him always."

"Of course," he attempted to soothe her. "Well, I won't keep you now and we'll figure something out. Don't worry. And when you need me —"

He let himself out of the house and got into his car, thinking of the flame that had ignited behind Carol Brindle's eyes. Roger's second wife had always reminded him of a long-haired cat, lovely to look at, soft to touch, with only a hint of hidden claws, with tawny hair and eyes so pale a brown they seemed to be yellow. Like a cat, Carol loved comfort; she was lazy and content and decorative and, he had assumed, with something of the untouchable nature of the Persian feline.

As he drove away, Griswold's sense of irreplaceable loss was lightened by the knowledge that Roger's young wife grieved for him, too.

Carol listened to the closing of the door and stood for a moment in the middle of the library, arms hanging limply at her sides, face so blank that it looked almost stupid. The uncharacteristic spark of anger was snuffed out and she felt empty. She was also alone.

She had been completely alone few times in her life. She should not have sent her niece to the Kibbees. The empty house was frightening. She caught herself on the verge of calling to Roger. But he was not there; he could not answer. He would never again fling open the front door and come in as though blown by a high wind, calling, "Where's my girl?"

At that moment Roger Brindle died for his wife. The house knew him no longer. The echo of his voice and his footsteps faded. There was only space and stillness — and finality. The numbness that had protected her rolled away like fog.

The shrill peal of the telephone startled her but she made no attempt to answer it. Go away, she said mentally, go away. But the person at the other end of the line was persistent and she walked on leaden feet to the telephone on the ornate desk that Roger had laughed at and never used. There were not many things on which he was adamant but his method of working was one of them.

"Hello."

Carol heard a series of clicks and distant voices speaking faintly to each other. She moved uneasily on the slippery red leather chair that was too big for her, that Roger had filled with his vibrant presence.

"This is Mrs. Roger Brindle."

The desk was piled with letters and telegrams. Roger will be busy, she thought, and checked herself. When would she be able to understand that Roger was dead? And that even close friends like Max Griswold dared to say the unforgivable thing, that she had not been first with him. Because there was no money. Only five thousand dollars. It might be a long time before she could touch even that small sum and all the expenses of the house going on meanwhile.

"I don't understand . . . who? . . . Mignonne? . . . Mignonne Franks . . . A literary agent? . . . Oh, I couldn't possibly. I can't write . . . A ghostwriter? . . . Ten thousand dollars!"

The crisp voice at the other end of the wire said, "You see, Mrs. Brindle, your husband had an immense and devoted following. They will be eager to know more about him as a man, those little personal touches no one would know as well as you. One of the leading weeklies will pay ten thousand for a series of four articles and there will undoubtedly be book publication afterwards. In fact, I think I can guarantee that. And there are people with the technical knowledge to help you with the writing. Mrs. Fleming, a client of mine, is available if you would like to discuss the matter with her. Of course, if you are absolutely determined against it, I will find someone else to write the articles."

Carol made up her mind without knowing she had done so. "No, I'll write them myself. Or at least — who is this ghostwriter?"

"Lois Fleming."

"I mean, is she a lady? That sounds snobbish, but would she fit in here?"

"She is entirely respectable." There was a hint of carefully controlled amusement in the distant voice. "A widow."

"Well — all right."

"Shall we say that Mrs. Fleming will be with you on the fifteenth?"

"The fifteenth," Carol agreed, feeling as though she had stepped off into deep water.

"I am sure," the literary agent said, "that it will prove to be a successful collaboration."

Carol set the phone back in its cradle, pushed aside the messages of condolence and remembered that Roger could not deal with them. A person does not die all at once, she realized then; but over and over, with every little habit, every place he has been, everything he has done.

She reached for the paper knife and began to open the telegrams and letters that told her, sometimes fluently, sometimes awkwardly, what Roger Brindle had meant to thousands of people whom he had never known.

"I feel that I have lost a personal friend. . . . He always called you 'my Carol' but you have been our Carol too. . . . The friends he talked about: Albert and Bessie, Joe and Ethel, good old Doc — we knew them all. . . . He came like a bright morning. . . . America's best-loved man."

Roger Brindle's widow read them and placed

them in a neat stack. Halfway through the pile she came upon a sheet of paper, without an envelope, without a signature. It read: "Died in his sleep — but how?"

TWO

Know what?" Bessie Kibbee removed her black hat and her good black dress, worn shiny at the seams. She was short and stout, with thin red hair and small eyes embedded like currants in a face as flat as a plate.

Albert Kibbee was propped high on pillows in the big double bed. He was a small man with a head that seemed too heavy for his scrawny neck. Wrists like pipe stems stuck out of the sleeves of his faded bathrobe. He lay staring at the ceiling and made no reply to his wife's comment. But Bessie Kibbee did not expect a response.

"It was a lovely funeral," she said with pleasure. "There's never been such flowers in this town. Some of them came all the way from New York. Just about the whole village turned out. Over sixty cars. And a beautiful sermon."

She cast a swift glance at her husband but his eyes still rested on the ceiling. There was no expression on his face. With fierce tenderness she bustled to his side and smoothed the sheet over him.

"Know what?" she repeated, but not hopefully. Albert never really cared about any of the small gossip she brought home to him as a lover might bring an offering of flowers. "Know who was at the funeral? Jane Brindle."

Albert's eyes left the ceiling, sought his wife's face. "Jane?" he repeated.

She nodded, delighted at having wrested him from his absorption, from the meditations that excluded her, that after more than twenty years of marriage kept her continually aware that the twain had never become one, that they were separate entities. Not all her profound love had been able to make a bridge between them. She said brightly, "She asked for you. First thing she said was, 'How's Albert?' And she wants to see you."

He pulled himself higher on the pillows, a faint tinge of color in his sallow face. "No! I won't see her."

Bessie Kibbee had given everything she had to her husband but she had learned nothing from marriage. So now she protested, "But after all these years —"

"No!"

"Anyone would think, to listen to you, Jane was a monster. And, except for being stouter and a little gray, she's just the same as she ever was. Know what? When I stood at the cemetery and watched Roger's two wives I couldn't help thinking he made a poor exchange. Of course, Carol's younger and she has a pretty face and I guess that's all a man cares about. Some men," she added hastily, her hand closing over Albert's thin arm. "But Jane —" she made a helpless gesture. "Jane is wonderful," she said simply.

Albert drew his arm away. "She never believed in Roger," he said in his reedy voice. "She was destroying him. From the beginning, Carol knew what he was; she helped him believe in himself. Just because the woman is pretty —"

Bessie snorted. "Think I'm jealous? At my age?" Hatred filled her mouth with a bitter taste. "Why Roger was so marvelous, why everyone had to believe in him as though he was God — there's times, Albert, when it's made me downright sick at my stomach to see you worshiping a man who wasn't worth tying your shoelace."

"Bessie!" The little man sat bolt upright, so frail that only the flame of the candle was left.

"All right," she capitulated, helping him to lie down again. "All right, dear. Not another word. I won't say another word. Though just the same —" she swallowed the words as though they choked her and summoned up a reassuring smile.

"I'm going to get up," Albert said. "What have you done with my clothes?"

"You can't have them. Just a few more days. You haven't eaten enough to keep up your strength."

She stood beside him, wearing a corset and stockings pulled tight over heavy legs. She put on a slip and a housedress, her voice coming muffled from the folds around her head.

"Know what? I brought Paula Case back with me for the rest of the day. Carol wanted to be alone and she let Clyde take Paula out for a drive in the car. It will give him a chance to get better acquainted with her. I suppose you've noticed how he feels about her."

"About Carol's little niece?" Albert said.

His wife gave a little cluck of exasperation. "Sometimes I think you're so wrapped up in your thoughts, Albert Kibbee, you don't know what is going on. That son of yours is head over heels in love with Paula."

Albert made no comment but Bessie was accustomed to that. "I suppose we've got to expect it," she went on. "He's the age to fall in love, and especially when he's just out of the army. Restless. And maybe it would be best for him to settle down. But we've had him so little." Her head emerged from the dress, she straightened the skirt. "At least, you'll have a chance now to talk more to him. Now he's grown up you'll find how — gentle he is. Of course, if he was to marry and live around here —" she broke off, her lips parted. "Albert! I hadn't thought of it before. What will happen to us now that Roger is gone?"

"The Lord will provide," he said gently.

She sat on the foot of his bed. "I suppose he left you something in his will. He was bound to do that. I'll say one thing for him, he always looked out for us."

"Did you see him?" Albert asked, following a track of his own.

"Who?"

"Roger. Before —"

"Yes, he looked natural; like he was asleep."

"Did he look happy?" When his wife made no reply Albert repeated his question with a touch of impatience.

"I was just thinking," she said in a tone of surprise, "I don't believe I ever saw Roger look really happy. Eager, of course. But — I don't know — lately he looked anxious. I wouldn't wonder if he was worried for fear Carol might find out about that Hattery woman. Anyone with an eye in his head could tell what was going on there. Him and his peerless secretary!"

"Roger was sorry for Ethel Hattery," Albert reproved his wife. "That's all there ever was to it."

There was a knowing gleam in Bessie's small eyes. "No man's pity made her blossom the way she did. The wonder is that Joe Hattery didn't suspect. Well, it's all water over the dam now. I hope Carol will get rid of them both."

ii

"I wonder," Joe Hattery said, "what happens to us now Mr. Brindle is dead. I don't suppose his wife will care. We could starve for all —"

"You might," Shandy Stowe suggested, "try working for a change." The black suit he had worn to the funeral was replaced by navy blue slacks and a maroon pullover. He hung the suit in the closet, walking with a faint halt that was not quite a limp. In a mirror set in the closet

21

door he looked automatically at the scars on his face and saw the reflection of Joe Hattery lurking behind him.

The ex-convict was slight and colorless, with a mouth that dipped steeply downward at the corners from chronic discontent and eyes that met one with an insistent candor which would not have deceived a child. The world was against Joe. It had always been against him. He never had any luck. If he didn't keep a sharp lookout to protect his rights, and Joe was extremely tender of his rights, he would be taken advantage of. His mother, who had been victimized as Joe had been, made all this clear to him before he was ten years old and he had seen no reason to change his mind in the next thirty years.

"Work," he whined now. "It takes a guy who never did a stroke of work in his life to say that. All right for one who's born with a silver spoon in his mouth to talk about other people working."

"Scram," Shandy Stowe said. "And next time knock before you come in this cottage."

"My, aren't we haughty!" There was a subtle change in Joe's voice. "You got no call to talk to me like that."

"Oh, get out," Shandy said wearily.

"Not yet, Mr. Stowe." Joe's stance, like his voice, had altered. He was not lounging now. "I got my own way of working. See?"

"Then go do it."

"Like replacing that windowpane in Mr. Brindle's cottage."

Shandy's eyes, which had gone compulsively to the scars on his face, narrowed with attention.

Joe grinned, revealing neglected teeth. "Interested in windowpanes? I've got one for sale."

"What the hell are you getting at?"

"I was just thinking, Mr. Brindle sure slept sound. Never woke up for no visitors even. I seen one of them go to his cottage that night myself." Joe took courage from Shandy's stillness. "Yessir, you could almost say the poor guy died of sleeping."

He broke off as there was a tap on the outside door and a woman called, "Shandy! Are you there?"

Carol Brindle, her tawny hair aglow in the sunshine, wearing a somber black dress, came swiftly across the living room of the cottage, her high heels clicking on the waxed floor. There was not a trace of her usual languor. Joe's eyes went from the woman to the man. He permitted himself a smirk as he went out.

"What is it, Carol?"

When she was seated, Shandy let himself down slowly into a chair facing her. He was surprised to discover that he was shaking.

Mutely she held out a piece of paper. "I just found this."

Shandy read it aloud, " 'Died in his sleep — but how?' Where, in God's name, did you get this?"

"On the desk in the library, in the middle of a pile of letters and telegrams of sympathy."

23

"Where's the envelope?"

"There wasn't any." Her eyes were wide with shock. "What ought I to do, Shandy? This could be — unpleasant, couldn't it?"

There was irony in his expression and something else which she failed to identify. "It could be, but probably it's just the work of a crackpot. Try to put it out of your mind."

"But you don't understand." Her eyes, which were so nearly yellow, gleamed. Her hair caught red and gold lights. She leaned forward, moving with the lovely supple rhythm of a cat. "You don't understand. Clyde locked everything before we left for the —" she skirted neatly the word that had such finality — "the services. No outsider could possibly have got in. And no one came to the house this morning but Doc Thomas and his wife. So it has to be —"

Shandy's voice was quiet. "One of us."

"And I don't know what to do. Roger always told me what to do."

"Not always," he reminded her. "You had a few ideas of your own."

She swayed toward him, her voice husky. "When I think what I have done to you! You've never really forgiven me, have you, Shandy?"

"On the contrary, I never blamed you."

"Roger," she said obliquely, as though answering some unspoken comment, "was the finest man I've ever known."

"At least," Shandy said, "he has a chance to get a long rest from it now. Being the finest —

it must have been a strain at times, even for Roger."

Carol frowned, and with the smooth forehead puckered she looked almost ugly for a moment. "Do you think it is wise to say things like that?"

"Perhaps not," he agreed. "But only Roger could be wise all the time." He reached out and took the anonymous letter that she was twisting between her fingers. "Better let me have that. Who put the mail on Roger's desk?"

"Clyde Kibbee."

"Clyde," he said thoughtfully. "I'll ask him about it." Seeing the look of alarm on her face he added, "Tactfully, of course."

"But how could Clyde possibly have known?" Carol demanded, and then said with feverish haste, "I mean, we don't know much about him, after all. He's been away at school since he was a small boy and even vacations he spent at camp because Albert was always unsettled. We don't really know what kind of person he might be. Somehow, he's not at all the sort of son you'd expect Albert to have. Just because he is Albert Kibbee's son doesn't mean he's — harmless, like Albert."

Shandy was silent for a long time. The woman watched the fading scars become suddenly sharp on his cheeks. His jaw had a rigid look as though his teeth were clamped hard together. At length he said noncommittally, "We don't know what kind of person anyone might be." Their eyes met and then they looked away. "Carol, why don't you take a trip somewhere, go off for awhile?"

"No money," she said briefly. "My lawyer was just here. Roger left only five thousand dollars and I don't even know when I can touch that."

"If I can help — but you know that."

"Yes, I know. I can't imagine what I would do without you, Shandy." She waited for a reply which did not come. She stirred uneasily. "I'm glad I never had to find out. And yet — why you go on living in this place when you could afford to live anywhere —"

Her eyes demanded an answer. Shandy looked around. "What's the matter with this?"

Her mouth twisted. Carol was accustomed to having her demands met immediately and Shandy was proving difficult. "You've let vines grow up around the windows. Your furniture is scuffed and it needs to be reupholstered. The whole cottage should be done over, repainted, refurnished."

He said indifferently, "I hadn't noticed. You are probably right."

"I'll redecorate it for you," she offered eagerly.

His dark eyes searched her face with alert speculation and then they were opaque again. "Let's worry about your problems, Carol, not about mine. We've got to solve your money difficulties first. How much —"

Carol leaned back in the big chair, one hand plucking at the worn slipcover. Shandy watched her through half-closed eyes. For the first time in her life she was driven to thinking. Always before she had evaded the unpleasant. He wondered how she would cope with it now. He was pleased to find that, in spite of the strength of her physical attraction for him, he could watch her with detachment.

"Later," she said. "But in a little place like this — if I took money from you now — the way the people in the bank talk — and someone would be bound to be — unkind."

The impassive face revealed none of his grim amusement.

"Anyhow," she went on, "a woman called me. A literary agent. She offered me ten thousand dollars to write some articles about Roger."

For a moment Shandy enjoyed the thought of Carol Brindle writing articles. "That would be a big job," he cautioned her.

"That or another," she said almost angrily. "I tell you there's nothing left. Roger squandered everything he had on all these worthless —" She became aware of the unpleasant sound of her own voice and automatically it became soft and lazy again. "Anyhow, they'll send a woman on the fifteenth to help me get it all down. She's a widow and very respectable but I don't want a stranger prying around the house just now."

Shandy's eyes opened wide and closed quickly. "She might be company for you."

The yellow eyes were on his face now, fixed and unblinking like a cat's. "I was hoping you'd be that," she said plainly. "Mrs. Fleming would just be an outsider."

27

"Who?" Shandy's face stiffened although his voice did not lose its detachment.

"Mrs. Lois Fleming. You know, Shandy, I think I'll put her in Roger's cottage. She'll be out of the way there and it would be morbid to keep the place locked up. As soon as — when they took — Roger away I locked the door. But if I leave it like that it will be haunted by — his death. And, anyhow, it will have to be — put in order. After a stranger has lived there for awhile it will be easier to go back; the place will have different associations." A long shudder ran down her body. She got to her feet, her eyes on the crumpled sheet of paper in his hand. "Are you sure it is all right?"

He did not look at her. "I'll handle it."

"Who did it? Who — wondered about the way he died?"

"God knows."

"No one could — make any trouble, could they?"

As the color ebbed from his face the scars appeared again. "There's nothing to be afraid of. Doc Thomas is in love with you, or didn't you know?"

She smiled faintly. "I guessed." She rested her tawny head against him. "Shandy." Her voice was muffled against his chest. Her hands clutched at him. His arms hung at his sides. She stepped back.

For a moment she was a blurred figure in the doorway against the brilliant sun and then she

28

walked across the wide lawn toward the gracious white house, a slim, black-robed woman moving with feline grace.

Shandy watched until the side door of the house closed behind her, his right hand deep in his pocket, clenched around the crumpled message. Then he too went outside, but not across the stretch of emerald green lawn. He plunged into the trees that climbed a hill behind his cottage. When he was tired tramping, he sat on the stump of a tree and looked down through a clearing onto the white colonial house set in its deep lawn, with four small cottages scattered over the grounds. And beyond was the village with its slim church spire thrusting up among the trees.

Lo-is Flem-ing. The syllables beat remorselessly on Shandy's nerves, like the ticking of a noisy clock, the dripping of water from a faucet. Lo-is Flem-ing.

How long was it since he had seen her, heard from her? Six years? Seven? The government had assigned him to help her find her husband who was reported missing and who had in his possession essential information. They had never got that information; instead, they had learned how well he had kept it and how horribly he had died to protect it. Even then, with the barrier of the man's appalling death between them, with a fiancée of his own awaiting him, he had known that what he felt for her he could feel for no other woman. Even then he had known what the future could be if he were to meet her under

29

other circumstances. Now at last she was coming. He found a grim humor in the situation.

"Kismet," said Shandy Stowe.

"He tried too hard," Lois declared. "And toward the end, those last few months, his column depressed me horribly."

Mignonne's eyes flickered. "That's a peculiar thing to say about one of the few genuine rock-bottom optimists writing in our time."

"But, you see," Lois said as though it must be obvious to everyone, "he didn't believe in it any more. He didn't believe in anything."

Mignonne leaned suddenly to reach for papers in the bottom drawer of her desk. She spoke with her face still hidden.

"What did you say?" Lois asked.

"A divining rod. You. What is it? This thing they call empathy?"

"There isn't anything," Lois said uneasily.

"Of course not. I was just joking. I'll put an informal agreement in the mail tonight for Mrs. Brindle and you get your clothes together so you can leave day after tomorrow."

"But that's only the fifth!"

"Exactly."

"You told Mrs. Brindle the fifteenth. I won't be expected."

"Exactly," Mignonne said again.

ii

"Stoweville!"

For a moment Lois Fleming stood on the platform, breathing in the sweet cool air, looking

35

at the rolling line of the Connecticut hills, at the trees — maple and oak, white birch and hemlock. Stoweville was better than she had expected.

"A typical New England village with a green." That was all Shandy Stowe had ever said to her of the little town that had been named for his great-great-grandfather. He had talked more about the house in which four generations of his family had been born. "A big white house with pillars, southern colonial in style, with ornate iron gates and four little cottages scattered around the grounds that have been added from time to time for guests." Strange how clearly she remembered.

There was no one to meet her, of course. She was not expected for another ten days. Serve her right if she were turned away at the door. For the first time she wondered why Mignonne had wanted her to make an unheralded appearance. Since her illness, she reflected, she had been putty in the hands of well-meaning relatives with whims of iron, of anyone who took a strong line about her. And Mignonne had taken a very strong line. She had been determined that Lois should accept this job.

Probably, Lois reflected ruefully, she knew I was still too dim to think for myself. Or was it that? It occurred to her now that Mignonne had been unlike her forthright self during that interview in her office. She had not really given Lois time to think about the job.

Lois stood uncertainly on the platform and then hailed the only taxi. "Mrs. Roger Brindle's home.

Do you know where it is?"

The driver swiveled around for another look at her. "Going to visit Mrs. Brindle, are you? Poor soul. It will do her good to have some company. That house without Mr. Brindle —" he shook his head dolorously.

Automatically, Lois found herself opening up a source of information on her subject. "Did you know him?"

"Everyone knew him. I guess it's not too much to say everyone loved him. Always a nice word and a smile for you. Of course, he lived here most of his life. Even after he was famous he wouldn't live anywhere else."

Something of Roger's shadow seemed to fall over the cab. How big he had been, Lois thought. He had filled this town with his presence. In a sense, he still filled it.

The taxi driver turned onto the village green, driving through the cool shade of great elm trees. Beyond were green lawns, towering trees, white houses self-consciously gleaming with an anxious eye for the public, criss-cross curtains crisp at sparkling windows. They passed a white church with a soaring spire, a red-brick town hall, a couple of houses with plaques telling of their historical place in the community, a mean street with shabby houses and filling stations; then a two-lane winding road with trees on either side and at the curves a distant view of low blue hills.

A quarter of a mile beyond the village the driver

slowed down before ornate iron gates through which Lois saw a deep lawn shaded by big elms and sugar maples and, some distance back from the road, a gracious colonial house with a beautiful doorway and a slender balcony supported by white pillars.

"But this must be the Stowe house!"

"It was," the driver said. "Mr. Stowe sold the place to Mr. Brindle right after he came back from the war. Just shut himself up like a hermit. People have almost forgotten that he still lives around here."

As he turned the car into the driveway Lois was thoughtful. This was the home to which Shandy had expected to take his bride. Something must have happened; the thing, perhaps, that he had anticipated and she had refused to believe possible. How vile, she thought in swift anger, how utterly vile. What kind of woman would break her engagement because a man had been scarred by war?

She stood on the porch for some time after she had paid off the driver, her luggage stacked neatly beside her. Then she took a deep breath and rang the bell. The door was opened by a young girl in black slacks and a yellow pullover who looked in surprise from Lois to the matching luggage.

"I am Mrs. Fleming," Lois said. "Mrs. Brindle is expecting me."

"Mrs. Fleming?" The girl stared at her in consternation. Then she stepped back awkwardly.

"I'm sorry. We thought you were coming on the fifteenth."

"What a shame."

"Sit down, won't you? I'll go get Aunt Carol. Oh, I'm Mrs. Brindle's niece, Paula Case." She was slight, with sandy hair and a sprinkling of freckles over her small nose. She was not pretty but she had the touching, ephemeral charm of seventeen. "I hope," she added politely, in an endeavor to cover the embarrassment of the unexpected arrival, "you aren't too tired from your trip."

As the train time from New York City was well under three hours, Lois was staggered. Then she recalled that Scott Fitzgerald as an undergraduate had written of "a fading but still lovely woman of twenty-eight."

"Nothing that a nice cup of tea won't cure," she said sedately, her eyes sparkling. "How lovely it is here!"

"The village green is quaint, if you like that sort of thing." There was a touch of condescension in the girl's voice. "And there are a lot of real characters around. Old-timers. Roger —" the young voice broke and then steadied, "Roger liked them."

Lois gave her a quick look. She saw now that there were shadows under the hazel eyes with their sandy lashes.

"Well," Paula said, backing away, "if you'll excuse me, I'll get Aunt Carol." She ran up the stairs as though eager to escape.

Lois looked around her. The first sharp impression of a man's house often told her as much about him as her first sight of the man himself. If she could not see Roger Brindle, at least she could see the surroundings in which he had lived. But, she reminded herself, this was not Roger Brindle's house, it was Shandy Stowe's.

Her strongest impression was that the house reflected two opposing personalities and had failed to blend them into a harmonious whole. A curving stairway with a mahogany banister, so exquisitely proportioned that it seemed to float in space, rose from the big hallway. Over the balcony railing hung a heavy tapestry, which was lovely in its own way, but made a curious impression of weighing down the soaring line, clipping the wings of a thing in flight.

On the left was a library with book-lined walls to which Lois gravitated like a needle to the north. Leather-bound sets of Dickens and Trollope, Darwin and Spencer, the Lake poets, a set of Greek and Latin classics in translation, fine editions of standard works. The successful man's library, bought by the yard, she thought. On a lower shelf were dog-eared essays of Emerson and Stevenson's "Home Book of Quotations." The latter had been read and re-read. The others had only been dusted.

She turned back to the hallway as Paula came breathlessly down the stairs.

"Aunt Carol is so sorry the cottage isn't ready for you, but it will be fixed up this afternoon.

I'll take you there now so you can unpack. Aunt Carol doesn't usually get up much before noon, but she said to tell you she's looking forward to meeting you at lunch at one o'clock." She got this message off in one breath and then opened the door and called shrilly, "Clyde!"

In a few moments a gangling young man, who was acquiring a permanent stoop in an effort to look smaller than he was, came in. Lois was the kind of person who could not sit near the stage at concerts because she suffered all the tortures of the musician's stage fright. This young giant was so agonizingly shy that a visible aura of his suffering seemed to her to engulf him like a cloud.

He was awkward, as though he had never learned how to manage so much in the way of arms and legs. He had a homely face, red hair and level eyes that brushed Paula Case briefly in a mingling of hope and doubt.

The girl made a peremptory gesture. "Take Mrs. Fleming's bags up to the cottage."

He gave Lois a swift glance and then said, "Okay, Paula. Give me the key and I'll open the cottage for you."

The girl observed Lois's surprise. "Oh," she said carelessly, "Mrs. Fleming, this is Clyde Kibbee."

"Kibbee!" Lois exclaimed in her warm, friendly voice. "But I didn't know that Albert and Bessie had a son."

The boy flushed brick red and Lois, torn between an instinctive desire to make him feel at ease and a woman's instinctive impatience with a man who needs so much reassurance, said, "Please don't think I am impertinent when I speak of Albert and Bessie. But I've read about them so long. You must have some of the best-known parents in America."

"And the nicest," he said gravely. He went out on the porch and gathered up the luggage, suitcases, hatbox, cosmetic case and typewriter.

"Well," Paula said uncertainly, "I guess you might as well see the cottage anyhow." She led the way along the path Clyde Kibbee had taken, skirting the garage and plunging into the woods.

"Um, cool," Lois said gratefully as they stepped into the dark shadow of the trees. "After New York this is heaven."

"I'm afraid the place will seem awfully neglected. Aunt Carol is giving you Roger's cottage, the one he worked in. It — no one has been inside since he died. Aunt Carol just locked the door. We couldn't bear —" she broke off again, her sandy lashes bright with tears.

She is too tense, too high strung, Lois thought. I do hope I haven't run into a case of incipient hysteria.

As though aware of Lois's thought, the girl defended herself. "It's only ten days since he died. You can't get used to it in ten days. He was — Roger made everything seem wonderful. I can't explain but I hope you'll be able to get that into what you write about him. Aunt Carol might not tell you things like that about him, things that didn't concern herself."

The girl licked her lips nervously but there was malice in her face as she watched furtively for Lois's reaction.

The cottage was almost hidden in the trees. Clyde unlocked the door and set Lois's bags down in the middle of the room. For a moment both he and Paula stood looking around them with unconcealed, avid curiosity.

Lois's first impressions were of air that was chilly and stale, of a faint ghost of an odor which was familiar but which she failed to identify, of furniture in disorder, of a windowpane starred as though someone had thrown a rock at it, and some adhesive tape fastened over the small hole.

Paula gave a sharp exclamation. "The window hasn't been repaired. I'm terribly sorry. Clyde, tell Joe Hattery to put in a new pane at once."

There was a big pine-paneled workroom with a small gas fireplace, comfortable wing chairs with good reading lights, a deep nine-foot couch whose down pillows still bore the impression of a head, two walls lined with books in their bright dust jackets, and a workmanlike unpainted table with a battered typewriter case and a stack of copy paper weighted down by an overflowing ashtray. At one side there was a small compact bathroom. The cottage had the air of a place that had been abandoned in a hurry.

A Dutch door in the back wall looked out on a small terrace enclosed by a twelve-foot fence in which a gate was set.

"Roger used the terrace for sunbathing," Paula explained. "That's why he had to build the fence. His admirers would do the strangest things. The gate is locked but your door key opens it. If you want to get out that way you'll have to unlock the gate because it locks itself automatically." She looked around. "There's a phone here, they're all over the place. You'll find the numbers tacked up on the wall."

She began to edge toward the door. "Well, I guess if there's nothing else —" She lingered and Lois thought, I do wish the young did not think they had gone when they have said good-by.

Paula pointed to a green cottage. "The Kibbees live there." Beyond was a gray stone cottage with a small shed attached to it. "The Hatterys have that one." Halfway up the hill, set in the woods, huddled a tiny white salt box. "Shandy Stowe lives there."

"Shandy!" Lois was thunderstruck.

"Oh, do you know him?"

"I did. Years ago."

"When he sold the place he kept that cottage for himself. A regular hermit but swell looking, isn't he? I like to see a distinguished looking older man."

Shandy, Lois reflected, must be a tottering old man of at least thirty-six.

Paula shook back her lank hair. "Clyde," her voice was sharp whenever she addressed the infatuated youth, "tell Ethel Hattery to clean up this cottage. She might as well do something to earn her keep."

Kibbee. Hattery. How familiar these names were, Lois thought. Roger Brindle had written of them until they were better known than one's neighbors.

"Ethel Hattery. She was his secretary, wasn't she?"

"She was." Paula's tone was acid. "But right now she's just a parasite. This place is overflowing with Roger's deadbeats."

Clyde's fair skin burned scarlet and then the color drained out, leaving it white. He left the cottage without a word. As Paula looked after him her expression was contrite.

"I suppose I shouldn't have said that. After all, he's just home from the army and it's not his fault if his father won't earn a living. Well," as Lois began to unpack, "I guess I'll go up to the house. Lunch is at one o'clock."

When the girl had gone, Lois looked around at Roger Brindle's cottage. Already the air was warmer, less dead, and the faint odor that had been trapped in the closed room was gone.

There was a creak as the gate in the fence opened and footsteps on the stone terrace. A man leaned over the half-open Dutch door, smiling at her.

It was Shandy Stowe.

FOUR

In the first glad flash of recognition he was not the Shandy of that long trip in search of her husband, with its final horrifying revelation. He was the Shandy of a single evening in a storybook German town with a castle whose crumbling tower they had climbed to look down on a tiny section of Europe unbelievably untouched by war. The setting had been to blame — unreal, remote, lovely — the setting and their youth and loneliness. Something, at least, must account for that strange interlude of passion that for an hour might almost have been love, that perhaps was love.

The man in the doorway turned and he was neither the Shandy whom she had so nearly loved nor the ingenious and light-hearted companion who had taken her to her journey's end. He was a stranger. Distinguished looking older man, Paula had said. Distinguished, yes. Older, yes. The sun touched his bronzed face, revealing faint white lines that were less scars than the memory of scars. But the alteration was deeper than the faded scars. The face that had been mobile was impassive, the mouth that had been sensitive was bitter, the eyes that had been candid were opaque. She could not see behind their shining surface.

"Hello, Lois," he said and opened the door

and came in, walking with a faint halt in his gait.

She held out both hands. "Shandy! How wonderful. When my agent said Stoweville, I hoped perhaps you still lived here."

"Did you?" he said and Lois flushed. He was amused by her confusion. "Why?" he asked reasonably. "I remind you of the appalling search we made for your husband, of finding where and how he died."

Lois was surprised to find that the words had lost their power to give her pain. She had loved her husband; with the help of Shandy, lent by a grateful government, she had hunted for him and relived his hideous death over and over. But it was done now, a gentle sorrow, and his face had faded little by little. It belonged to the past.

"I am really glad to see you," she assured him.

"Mrs. Brindle told me you were coming." He stood with his head cocked a little on one side, seeing the changes that seven years had made in her. "You're prettier, if anything, because you are more relaxed. And you still stand as if poised for flight. What gives you that winged quality?" He did not wait for an answer. "And you haven't lost that bright-eyed curiosity of yours. I always felt you should have been in Intelligence, not I. As I remember, the muscles were supplied by me but you had the —" he considered — "intuition?" he asked as though uncertain.

He doesn't like me, Lois thought, brushing

aside his words to get at his meaning.

"I hear you are a real live ghost." He added unexpectedly, "Why are you?"

Lois pushed back her hair with an impatient gesture as familiar to him as his own face in the mirror. "Why am I a ghost?" She grinned at him. "Our motto is, 'Take the cash and let the credit go.' I needed the cash."

"Badly enough to bring you here ten days ahead of time?" His eyes raked her face. "Catching us unprepared."

A wave of anger swept over her, anger at Mignonne who had put her in this predicament, at Shandy for the hostility he revealed fleetingly, most of all at herself for minding so much, for discovering that Shandy had this power to wound her.

"I'm sorry if my blunder has made things awkward," she said lightly. "I don't know how I happened to do such a thing. I'm the kind of woman who goes to a dinner party on the wrong night."

Shandy dismissed this and went back to the point that interested him most. "Do you use that intuition of yours in ghosting?"

"Oh, don't be ridiculous! Ghostwriting is merely telling another person's experience as he would tell it if he were trained. There's too much nonsense about it. People who live at first hand don't often have a talent for communicating experience. The Churchills are rare birds. After all, writing is a craft like any other. There's no more

48

reason that a doctor or a lawyer or a politician or an explorer should be a writer than that he should be a musician. An honest ghost reflects his subject. That's all there is to it."

"But he also has to understand him."

"That, of course. Ghosting is as old as the written word. Our own George Washington was ghosted. Dumas had a whole stable of ghosts and everyone knew it. Once he asked a friend if he had read the latest Dumas novel and the friend replied, 'No, have you?' "

Shandy was still studying her. "You have been ill," he said, and there was more friendliness in his voice.

Pneumonia, she told him. She was all right now except that she had not quite picked up her strength. A few weeks of country air ought to do the trick.

His eyes went around the room with the same avid curiosity she had observed in Paula and Clyde, moving slowly, scanning it foot by foot. Aware that she was watching him, he grumbled, "They haven't fixed the place up. That cracked windowpane should have been removed. They haven't even emptied the ashtrays."

He walked across the floor, his steps faintly uneven, and shook up the pillows on the long couch which still held the impression of Roger Brindle's head, as though driving from the cottage the last vestige of the man's presence. The simple gesture seemed queerly ruthless. Something dropped to the floor as he moved the cushions, something that had lodged in the frame of the couch.

Outside the window a shadow moved and Lois started. Her nerves still weren't what they might be, she thought, and there had been a furtive quality about that movement.

Shandy said, "Joe Hattery has come to replace the windowpane. And high time. With the place locked up, nothing could be done before."

They watched while the small man outside scraped putty and lifted the glass onto the ground, taking quick sidelong looks at Lois and Shandy and around the cottage. When he had gone, Shandy said, "Carol asked me to bring you to lunch. It's a bit early but let's get out of here and walk for awhile."

Lois opened her handbag and collected a handkerchief, cigarettes and compact. When she looked up, Shandy was holding the door open for her and the thing that had dropped from the couch was gone, the thing that looked like a bullet.

Shandy steered her around the side of the cottage. Questions hovered on her lips. She wanted to know why he had sold the house he loved and now lived "like a hermit." She wanted to know why he had not married the girl to whom he had been engaged seven years before, the girl to whom he had been afraid to return because of what the war had done to him: his lameness, his mutilated face. And she dared not ask her questions of the stranger he had become.

They strolled out of the scalding heat of the

sun into the shade of the woods. As they passed the stone cottage that belonged to the Hatterys they heard someone moving in the shed beyond. Lois had a curious impression that Shandy shied away; then he turned deliberately and looked in at the open door. A woman with flaxen braids wound around her head, a shabby skirt with an irregular hem and a sweater with holes in it, stood looking down, in her hand a forgotten cigarette from which the smoke was spiraling.

Lois followed the eyes of the absorbed woman. She was looking at the broken pane of glass propped against the wall. Shandy moved and his shadow fell on the floor. Without turning around, the woman laid the windowpane on the ground, picked up a hammer, and deliberately smashed it.

ii

They had gone some distance, climbing up into the woods, before Shandy spoke. "That, of course, was Ethel Hattery, the faithful, the dependable, the noble secretary."

"I didn't know," Lois said irrelevantly, trying to reconcile Roger Brindle's word portrait with the living person, "that his secretary was pock-marked. Otherwise, she'd be rather pretty." As Shandy leaned forward to light her cigarette the sun fell on his face through a clearing between the trees. "I'm so glad your scars have all gone.

Of course, they were never as bad as you thought but it's wonderful to have them vanish almost without a trace."

His hand went to his face. He caught his breath.

"Didn't you know that yourself?" she asked, shocked by something she saw in his eyes.

"Oddly enough, I didn't."

"Is that," Lois demanded furiously, "why you have withdrawn into your shell like a turtle? Go home and take a look at yourself. Even Paula, who seems to think anyone over twenty-five is decrepit, described you as distinguished looking."

"Good girl," Shandy encouraged her in a mocking tone. "Stay right in there, pitching."

Lois closed her lips firmly on what she had been about to say. Shandy made no attempt to break the silence, seeming quite content to stroll beside her, listening to that deep concerted hum of insects which in midsummer sounds like the earth breathing. Seven years vanished as though they had never been. This might be that night when they had stood on a crumbling tower and turned to one another, wordlessly, as though the real goal of their journey were this refuge in each other's arms.

Shandy's voice was quiet. "Time is a curious thing, past and present all blended together."

His mind was following hers too closely for comfort, and she attempted to sidetrack him. "Shandy, tell me about these people."

"Tell you what?"

She was exasperated. "Honestly, what's come over you? You've grown as guarded and cautious as a lawyer. You know them well. In a few weeks I'll have to capture a picture of them but if they are as unexpected as Mrs. Hattery I'll be all mixed up, trying to reconcile the true picture with Roger Brindle's word picture."

"A true picture," he said thoughtfully. "It can't be done, you know. Set half a dozen painters to do a portrait and you'll get half a dozen different subjects. They'll all be true because each portrait represents what that particular painter really saw."

"But —"

"I knew a man once," he went on, "who made a hobby of sitting for artists: oil or watercolor, charcoal or pen and ink, etching or lithograph, sculpture chiseled out of marble or modeled in clay, academic or modern. They were a fascinating study because each of them was half a portrait of my friend and half a portrait of the artist. All of them were true and none of them."

With the care of one who lives in the woods he crumpled his cigarette before dropping it. "That's what you will find here, Lois. Everyone knew a different Roger Brindle."

"You mean the man was like a chameleon?"

"Not at all. He was consistent enough. They simply looked for different things because each one's need was different."

"What was he: all things to all men?"

"That about summed him up."

53

"What was your opinion of him, Shandy?" she asked directly.

After a pause he said, as though weighing his words, "I had nothing against him."

Lois waited but he did not seem to be aware that anything more was expected of him. "You aren't," she complained, "being very helpful."

"Your obedient servant, ma'am. What do you want to know?"

"For one thing, why did Mrs. Hattery deliberately smash that pane of glass?"

"Very likely because she was afraid." Shandy looked at his watch, making the gesture obvious. "I suppose we had better start back."

Lois dug her toe into the ground and stood with her head back, an air of unconscious challenge about her. Shandy felt that challenge in the squaring of her shoulders, the level of her chin.

"Afraid of what?"

"Afraid of curiosity," he told her and again she was aware that this man whom she had known so well had become a stranger.

"Mine?"

"Yours."

"Then it was a bullet," Lois said bluntly.

They came out of the woods, passed the cottage that had been Roger's, its window still boarded up, and crossed the velvet expanse of lawn toward the big white house that had once been Shandy's.

"What does it matter?" he said at length. "No one has been shot."

They went up the shallow steps to the deep veranda and he opened the door, stepping back for her to precede him. "No one bothers to ring here. You just walk in."

After the heat and brilliant sunshine the house was cool and shady, scented by huge Chinese vases filled with spicy potpourri.

Through the arch to the drawing room, across the hall from the library, Lois could see a stout, middle-aged woman who was putting the finishing touches to the dining room table.

"Hello, Bessie," Shandy called.

She came through the drawing room, her small eyes fixed on Shandy.

"I haven't laid eyes on you in days," she commented. "I was saying to Albert only this morning it would take a fire to smoke you out. I tried to speak to you at Roger's funeral but you had your head down and your hat pulled over your eyes as though you were afraid someone would recognize you."

Shandy spoke hastily. "This is Mrs. Fleming," he said. "Mrs. Albert Kibbee."

Lois could not help a faint pang of disappointment. Roger Brindle's column was always referring to Albert and Bessie who had been his childhood friends: Albert the dreamer, Bessie the wife who anchored him to the ground with commonsense. He had made Bessie extremely funny and she was, after all, a drab sort of woman. No one would bother to look at her twice.

"Glad to meet you," Bessie said in a tone that

belied the words. She scrutinized the slim, dark-eyed woman with the curly hair and warm, eager face. "You the one who's going to write up Roger?"

"I'm going to help Mrs. Brindle."

"Hm. Going to get him all down on paper, are you?" For a moment there was a sardonic gleam in Bessie's small eyes.

"How is Albert?" Shandy asked her.

Bessie Kibbee made a fleeting gesture of helplessness. "He just lies there. I can't seem to stir him up. He's grieving himself to death."

"Better have Doc take a look at him."

Bessie snorted. "Doc Thomas is so busy trying to be the old family friend Roger made him out to be that he's got downright foolish. I take better care of Albert any day than he can — if I could just rouse him. But he shuts himself off, even from me. Taken to locking the door of his room. Know what, Shandy? Jane Brindle is back in Stoweville."

"Jane!"

She nodded with a cautious look toward the stairway. "If you didn't burrow like a mole you'd know it. The whole village is talking. She was at Roger's funeral. You'd have seen her if you hadn't stood off by yourself. She is staying at the inn. Well, you'll have to excuse me. Lunch won't put itself on the table the way some people seem to think."

When she had trotted back to the kitchen Lois looked up to find Shandy grinning at her. "So that is Bessie Kibbee," he said, using the words, the inflection, she had been about to use.

"It's the queerest experience," she said, feeling on the defensive without knowing why, "to meet people about whom I have read so often. Like opening a book and suddenly the landscape and the characters come to life. Only — naturally, you think you know what they are like and then —"

"Don't underestimate Bessie," Shandy warned her. "She's quite a girl."

"I just expected her to be more —"

"Quaint?"

In itself the irony in his voice would not have bothered her. But there was, as well, a latent hostility. She bit back a sharp response and said, "More colorful, perhaps. And I didn't know she was a kind of servant."

"No," Shandy said oddly, "you couldn't have known that."

FIVE

Carol Brindle came around the curve of the staircase, wearing a sheer black dress unrelieved by
any touch of color. Her tawny hair supplied all
the contrast she needed. Even when she saw them
she moved without haste. A graceful, glowing
woman. Again Lois revised her preconception.
"My Carol" had been a helpless creature, Dora
the child wife. This Carol was like a magnolia,
lush and lovely. But not childish, Lois thought.
Definitely not childish.

Judging by her expression, the widow was
equally unprepared for her collaborator. She had
expected thick glasses, dowdy clothes and ugly
legs, Lois thought in resignation. Only Edna St.
Vincent Millay ever made writing seem like a
glamorous craft for women.

"Mrs. Fleming, please forgive me for not wel-
coming you sooner and for being so stupid about
the date of your arrival. I'm desperately sorry.
No one to meet you at the station and the cottage
not in order. Since my great sorrow I've been
awfully vague."

Lois's reply was cut off by Bessie Kibbee who
stumped into the hall, her face flushed with heat.
"I've got a cheese soufflé. Do we have to wait
for anyone?"

But at that moment Carol's niece, Paula, came down the stairs; Clyde Kibbee emerged from the kitchen, stooping to avoid the top of the door; and they all, including Shandy, went in to lunch. Bessie's position seemed to be an odd one. She cooked and served the meal, which was superlative; she waited on them; but she joined them at the table. Occasionally, Lois observed that she was attempting, with a flat-footed obviousness that defeated its own purpose, to promote conversation between Paula and Clyde, but that her efforts made little headway against Paula's indifference and Clyde's agonizing shyness.

Shandy and Carol, with an occasional comment from Lois, carried the luncheon conversation, which for some reason proved to be heavy going. There were too many undercurrents. Lois, who had long since come to fear her sensitiveness to atmosphere, felt as though she had stepped into one of Eugene O'Neill's dramas of repression in New England, which was absurd in this gay, sunlit room. And yet it seemed to her that Paula was constantly watching her aunt without appearing to do so; that Shandy stiffened to alertness when Clyde Kibbee made one of his rare comments, which he did only when he thought he was least likely to be heard; that Bessie's small eyes darted from face to face when her son spoke, as though attempting to catch some fleeting hint of the impression he made.

"The Hatterys are putting the cottage in shape for you, Mrs. Fleming," Carol said at last. "I should have attended to it myself but I haven't been able to go inside since the morning when Clyde found Roger dead there. We simply locked it up and no one has set foot in it until today. We planned to open it next week for you."

"Oh," said Lois, taken aback. "I had not realized that Mr. Brindle died in the cottage."

Carol bit her lip. Then she said, "I hope that doesn't bother you."

How can you answer such a comment, Lois wondered. She was spared a reply because Paula said, "I told Ethel where to find clean blankets for Mrs. Fleming."

Carol smiled at Lois's expression. "Oh, yes, blankets. It gets cool at night. I only hope you won't find the cottage too chilly."

"The prospect is wonderful after New York," Lois assured her. "Anyhow, if I am uncomfortable, there's a gas fireplace. That ought to do the trick."

There was a curious silence.

"I — that is, we don't think gas is safe," Carol said at last. "Joe Hattery will take an electric heater up to the cottage for you."

"But I'm not in the least afraid," Lois assured her. "I have a gas fireplace in my New York apartment and there has never been the slightest difficulty."

"Still — you can depend on electricity. Joe will be glad to bring you a heater. He might as well be doing something." Young Mrs. Brindle turned to Shandy. "What on earth am I to do about the Hatterys? It was one thing when Roger was making a big salary, and at least Ethel was a fine secretary and worked hard; but now I simply can't support them. Anyhow, I've never been comfortable with Joe Hattery on the place. Say what you like, he's an ex-convict. Nothing better than a criminal. I don't think it is safe for Paula and me, alone in this big house. And when Paula goes —"

"I didn't know," Clyde began, startled into speech by his surprise, "that Paula was going away."

Carol raised her beautifully arched eyebrows. "Well, I —" she seemed to be embarrassed. "Perhaps I just jumped to conclusions. I used to hear her talking to Roger, so eager to get a job and be self-supporting. I remember — she even wanted to take Ethel Hattery's place."

Paula was crimson. She pushed back her chair. "It's all right with me," she said shrilly. "Perfectly all right with me. I always knew it was just Roger who wanted to give me a home, that you'd send me away as soon as you could."

"Paula!" Carol said reproachfully, not bothering to raise her voice.

"You can look innocent but it's not the first time you've tried to drive me out. Well, this time I'm going. You needn't worry. There's nothing to keep me now. You needn't go on pretending — you and your great sorrow!"

She stormed out of the room. They could hear her sobbing as she stumbled up the stairs and then the bang of a door.

"What will you think of us, Mrs. Fleming!" Carol exclaimed. "I can't imagine what's come over the child."

"She seems rather nervous," Lois said. "Girls of that age are apt to be a bit unstable emotionally." She longed to add, "What that little self-dramatizing exhibitionist needs is to be turned over someone's knee and paddled."

Shandy was pulling a piece of bread apart, crumbling it in his fingers, and Lois recalled having watched him do that one night in an Austrian farmhouse. Behind a flimsy door an armed man had waited and Lois's nerves were screaming. Shandy had continued to talk in an easy, casual way, his voice even, only his restless hands betraying his tension as he pulled at the bread and crumbled it.

To his mother's despair, Clyde had stopped eating. He looked as though he wanted to go in pursuit of Paula but did not quite know how.

"Another cinnamon bun," Bessie said anxiously, pushing the plate toward him. "Eat them while they're hot."

Clyde tried to smile at her and shook his head.

"But I thought you liked cinnamon buns. You used to eat all you could hold."

Carol went on in her soft voice. "Joe Hattery hasn't done a stroke of work since Roger died, and Ethel goes stalking around like Lady Macbeth. Anyone would think she was the widow. Shandy," she leaned forward, one ringed hand on his arm, "Shandy, do it for me, will you? Tell them to leave — in a nice way, of course."

Shandy's face tightened. "Do you think that's wise, Carol? There is nothing to be gained by antagonizing the Hatterys." He added quickly, "I think you are right, of course, to want to be rid of them. But let's see what we can figure out without actually throwing them off the place. Why don't I put an ad in the New York papers, saying that Roger Brindle's secretary is looking for another employer to whom she can be as useful as she was to him?"

Something in the inflection of his voice made Lois look from Shandy to Carol. There was an undercurrent of meaning that escaped her.

"Anyone who can read," Shandy went on blandly, "knows about Ethel the Faithful Secretary. That ought to bring her any number of good offers."

Lois shifted uneasily in her chair. In spite of the spontaneous manner in which Shandy made the suggestion, it sounded to her like something that had been rehearsed.

"What a wonderful idea! I'd never have thought of that." Carol's face clouded. "But would anyone else put up with her husband?"

"Joe," Shandy assured her, "is adept at being taken care of. If Ethel gets a good job he will have no objection. And if he knows what is good for him," Shandy's pleasant voice grew hard, "he'll learn to behave himself."

They had nearly finished luncheon when the

doorbell rang. Bessie got up and went to answer it. There was an exclamation, a murmur of voices, footsteps, and Bessie stood in the doorway between the dining room and the drawing room. Behind her was a tall woman with graying hair and a plain, charming face. Shandy got to his feet, a very odd expression on his face.

"Carol," Bessie Kibbee said, unable to control her excitement, "I guess you two ought to know each other. This is Jane Brindle, Roger's first wife."

ii

Carol looked with unconcealed curiosity at her predecessor. "I am so glad to see you," she said tranquilly.

"Forgive me for coming," said the lovely voice which was the older woman's only beauty.

"You couldn't have come at a better time. Because you knew Roger when he was young." Carol made the words sound light-years away. "I'm going to write his life story and I want to know about him when he was a boy. And anyhow," she added simply, "we have so much in common."

Lois saw Jane Brindle's big, ugly, humorous mouth twitch for a moment and felt her firm handclasp when Carol had performed the introductions. Jane gave her a keen glance that weighed her but was not unfriendly.

"Lois Fleming? Then we have a mutual acquaintance. Mignonne is my agent, too, and I've heard her mention you. Wonderful gal with articles, isn't she?"

Queer, Lois thought, she had never realized that the Jane Brindle who wrote articles had any relationship to Roger Brindle. Probably because their work was so utterly different, his warm and personal, hers brilliant and pungent but impersonal.

Jane brushed aside Carol's introduction of Shandy and kissed him exuberantly. "I've known this boy since he was five."

Shandy reached for a chair but Carol failed to suggest that the first Mrs. Brindle sit down. In the pleasantest possible way she was making clear that the older woman was an intruder in her home, an uninvited guest with no recognized status whatever. Jane Brindle, serene and poised, seemed totally unaware of her ungraciousness.

"Put on a bit of weight, haven't you?" Bessie commented.

Jane laughed. "Still the same old Bessie."

"You get no compliments from me. I say what I mean and I don't dress it up."

"It's outrageous for me to barge in like this," Jane declared. "How is Albert?"

"He's just pining away," Bessie told her. "Ever since Roger died. It's as though part of him had stopped living."

"Part of him did," Jane said quietly. "When can I see him?"

65

Bessie, always so forthright, was embarrassed. "I'll tell him you are here. But he won't see many people."

Carol Brindle was uneasy when she was not the focus of the conversation. She intervened now. "Albert is getting almost as difficult as Shandy. I sent for Dr. Thomas and he simply refused to let him enter the cottage."

"Albert's not himself. He hardly even talks with Clyde," Bessie said. "I guess you don't recognize Clyde, Jane. It must be umpteen years since you've seen him."

Jane ignored the touch of defiance in Bessie's voice and turned to the boy who had been studying her all this time, half expecting to be noticed, half prepared to be overlooked. Her smile grew a trifle stiff, as though she were holding it by main force.

"Clyde! I'd never have known you!" She made a quick recovery. "And small wonder. You were about eleven last time I saw you and still small enough so that I could look at you without a crick in my neck." She held out her hand to the boy and turned to Bessie who was watching her alertly. She smiled reassuringly down at the plump little woman.

The latter's face warmed, relaxed. "It's good having him here. He was away at school so long and then in the army — he'n Albert are just getting acquainted."

Jane's smile lighted her face. "I don't mind sharing Albert with you," she told the boy, "but

66

I won't let you monopolize him. Tell him he can't keep me out. If he locks the door I'll simply storm the windows."

"It would do him a world of good," Bessie declared. "Why he should go on resenting you because you divorced Roger, as though no one could pick a flaw in the man —" Vaguely she realized that she was being untactful. "You know how Albert is, just living in Roger. Never could see any of the fault might have been Roger's."

"Will you be here long, Jane?" Shandy intervened hastily.

Her eyes twinkled in her grave face. "Just a week or two. I'm giving myself a long-delayed vacation."

Lois was fascinated by the contrast between Roger's two wives. Carol's loveliness glowed in the room, soft and delicate and as pervasive as the perfume she wore. Jane was plain, with alert intelligence, considerable humor and a sturdy direct self-reliance.

"You're very successful, aren't you?" Carol asked her predecessor. "Roger used to speak of it when he saw your name signed to articles in big magazines. He was pleased to know you'd done so well." The soft voice acquired an edge. "You aren't planning to do any articles about Roger, are you, because I've been asked —"

Shandy's eyes brushed Lois's face, he winked at her, and looked away again. Implicit in the tiny gesture was shared amusement and understanding.

"No," Jane assured the embryo writer, "I won't do any articles about him."

"And if you have any material —" Carol began, determined not to waste an opportunity.

Jane's smile deepened. "If I have any material," she assured the younger woman, "I'll be happy to give it to Mrs. Fleming."

Lois swallowed hard. Jane too had claws, though it was doubtful whether Carol was astute enough to feel the scratch.

"Thanks for the lunch, Carol," Shandy said. "Jane, if you go away before I see you again I'll wring your neck."

"Don't be absurd," she said briskly, "I intend to ask you to take me to dinner."

"Tonight? Sold."

"Well," Carol exclaimed, "I'm glad there is something that will bring this caveman out of his retreat."

"Soon as I get those dishes cleared off," Bessie said to Jane, "I'll tell Albert you are here. Shake him out of himself. He says he's saving his strength so he can tell Mrs. Fleming all about Roger. Says no one knew him as he did."

"It was a nice lunch, Bessie," Carol said kindly. "Mrs. — it seems funny to call you Mrs. Brindle when that's my name — anyhow, I'm glad to have seen you. I always wondered what you were like." Her tone implied that she was quite satisfied on that score. "Mrs. Fleming, let's go into the library where we can talk. It's so much cooler there."

She nodded to Jane and laid her hand on Shandy's arm. "There are some scrapbooks of Roger's that are awfully heavy. Will you take them up to the cottage for Mrs. Fleming?"

"Glad to."

"Thanks, Shandy," Lois said absently, became aware of the stillness and knew that she had blundered.

He picked up the scrapbooks and went out. Carol stretched out on a long couch in the library and piled pillows behind her.

"I didn't know you and Shandy were acquainted."

"We met in Europe," Lois explained. "Years ago. Just after the war. Shandy was assigned by the government to look for my husband who was reported missing. He helped me find out — what had become of him."

"I knew he was delayed getting back because of looking for some man." The yellow eyes watched Lois without blinking. "But I've never heard him mention your name. When I told him you were coming he didn't even say he knew you."

"He'd probably forgotten all about it. You know how it is. You lose touch with people so easily. And I had no idea," Lois went on carefully, because it seemed important to make the point, "that I would meet him here. I had a vague idea he was married. Did his wife die?"

"Shandy never married," Carol said. Her eyes closed in sleepy satisfaction. "This was his old family home, you know. He sold it to Roger when we were married. I was crazy about the place so Roger was eager to get it for me. Roger was like that. Always. Sometimes I think his whole life was spent just in giving people what they wanted."

The young widow sat so absorbed in her thoughts that Lois hesitated to break in on them. Unexpectedly, Carol asked, "Do you think Shandy has changed much?"

SIX

Changed?" Lois echoed. For some reason she found herself weighing her words, moving cautiously as though testing each step to be sure of firm ground beneath. "Of course, he was badly scarred when I knew him and quite lame. The scars have almost vanished. I had no idea he was so strikingly good looking. And he's hardly lame at all, just a little stiff."

Carol was thoughtful. "Seeing him constantly, I guess I just hadn't noticed how his scars had disappeared. They were horrible at first, weren't they?" She shivered daintily to indicate her disgust.

Lois held an iron grip on her anger. "He'd had a rotten time of it," she said briefly.

Carol nodded. "He just turned into a regular hermit. If Roger hadn't routed him out by main force now and then he would never have left his cottage. But Roger — he couldn't stand having anyone unhappy. He'd just sweep them along with him. He was the strongest man I ever knew. Somehow I can't get it into my head that he won't come in, calling me, and say he'd just been away for awhile."

From the kitchen came the muted sounds of running water, the tinkle of silver, the scraping of kettles and the voices of women.

Carol stretched comfortably. "So that's Jane. I never pictured her like that. Roger was always so generous, never a word against her. He said she was a fine person. But I'd have expected her to be more attractive, wouldn't you? Do you think it's true that she won't write about Roger?"

"We have the same agent," Lois said. "She would never set us at conflicting jobs."

"I suppose not. Still, it's queer that Jane should come back here now unless she wants something. She hasn't been in Stoweville since the divorce and now she comes back just when Roger dies. I heard she was in town and at the — the services — though I didn't see her myself. Unless she thinks — but Roger didn't leave her a cent. Anyhow," Carol conceded, "I don't believe she is mercenary. She wouldn't accept a cent of alimony from Roger, though he felt awful about it."

She brooded for a moment. "I wonder just how Shandy will get out of taking her to dinner. He's never gone to public places since the war because of the way he looked. Getting him here to lunch was an achievement, I can tell you." Her voice changed. "Unless he wanted to see you again."

With a murmured excuse Lois got up to leave.

"I'm terribly sorry," Carol told her. "You know I made that idiotic mistake about the day you were coming and I'm dining with Dr. Thomas and his wife tonight. They wanted me to get away from the house and my great sorrow for a little while. So I've asked Bessie to fix you a

72

tray. Do you mind?"

Lois assured her that she did not mind in the least and went out into the broiling sun with a feeling of escape. She strolled up the path through the woods that led to her cottage, in the dark shade of the trees, watching a tiny orange lizard scramble over a minute twig.

There were voices at her cottage; evidently the Hatterys were at work. But when she came in sight of the place she saw that the voices belonged to Shandy Stowe and Joe Hattery.

". . . as a second offender," Shandy was saying.

"I'm not going back to prison. Nobody's going to railroad me."

"Nobody is trying to. But I warn you to drop this now."

"Yeah? I'm not dumb, Mr. Stowe, I got eyes and 20/20 vision."

"And a big mouth. Watch it, Hattery, or, by God, you'll be sorry you were born."

Hattery brushed off his hands with a gesture that was vaguely impertinent, faintly challenging. Then he straightened and saw Lois. Warned by his eyes, Shandy turned around.

"Hi there," he said cheerfully. "The Hatterys have the cottage nearly ready. Ethel has the place cleaned; she's getting fresh bedding and soap and towels. Joe will put that windowpane in for you and bring you an electric heater." He steered her quickly inside the house as though eager to get her out of Hattery's presence.

Already the cottage looked more cheerful. It

73

was spotlessly clean, the Dutch door was wide open. On the big worktable were piled a dozen or more heavy scrapbooks.

Shandy looked around dubiously. "Does it look all right? Anything more you need?"

"Thanks, it's fine."

"Sorry I can't kill the fatted calf for you tonight but Jane —"

"Of course."

He looked down at her with a faint smile. "Tomorrow, then. It's good to have you here; better than good. I never really expected to see you again. As though a chapter had ended. Or the whole damned book." For a moment he bent over as though he were going to kiss her; then he changed his mind and went quickly out of the cottage.

Lois lighted a cigarette, settled down at the oversized table that had been Roger Brindle's and arranged the scrapbooks in chronological order. They contained all his columns from the beginning, twenty years before, with one volume devoted to pictures. She opened this one first. It was, she discovered in surprise, simply an old-fashioned photograph album.

Each picture had been neatly dated with names printed underneath. The grim pair on the first page were Sarah and Jeremy Grant; Sarah, comic in leg of mutton sleeves, a large plumed hat and trailing skirt, was not comic in the thinness of her mouth, the flaring of her nostrils. She appeared to be the sister of Roger's father and it was she and her husband who had brought up the boy after the death of his parents. Not, Lois ruminated, a congenial home for a small child. Her agile imagination pictured the boy being sent back to close doors noiselessly, scraping his shoes before entering a spotless kitchen, being seen and not heard at table.

She studied carefully the pictures of Roger as a small boy, trying to learn something from the child he had been. He had always been homely, but even in group pictures, taken with other children, his was a face to which one turned back. He had the elusive, intangible thing called charm.

There was a sound of heavy breathing behind her and Lois, who had not heard a footstep, turned with a start. A woman with flaxen braids wrapped around her head and a pockmarked face was looking around the cottage as though seeking for something.

"I am Ethel Hattery," she said. "You must be Mrs. Fleming."

Lois held out her hand. "How do you do, Mrs. Hattery. I've looked forward to knowing you."

Ethel smiled faintly. "That's nice of you." She dropped a heap of linen and blankets on a chair. "The place will be ready as soon as the bed is made up. Then you won't be disturbed. I'm used to writers. Mr. Brindle didn't like to have anyone around when he was working."

Smallpox had left her skin pitted and doughy in texture but her features were good. Her eyes disturbed Lois. Hot eyes, she thought. A volcano.

She had a healthy distrust of unleashed emotion.

Ethel Hattery opened the big couch, made the bed, hung towels in the bathroom. Lois watched her. "Stalking around like Lady Macbeth," Carol Brindle had said, and had added resentfully, "as though she were the widow."

Not Lady Macbeth, Lois thought. Roger Brindle's secretary was a heroine straight out of one of the Brontë sisters. Not, Lois told herself, that she minded emotion, but she respected its control. If only people didn't pride themselves so on their emotional orgies.

Ethel returned and for a moment she stood beside the worktable. One hand touched it with a lingering caress.

"Perhaps," Lois suggested, "you will be willing to help me. Probably no one is as familiar with Mr. Brindle's method of work as you are. We'd be so grateful —"

"We!" Ethel's lips twisted in a wry grimace. "Any work that is done you'll do. Mrs. Brindle won't lift a finger if there's anyone to do it for her."

"Well," Lois said cheerfully, "that's what I'm here for."

"Don't you mind," Ethel asked, "when someone else gets the credit?"

Lois laughed. "That's the number one question asked of ghosts. The answer is no, I don't mind." She added in her warm, eager voice, "But do please think about it and let me know something about Mr. Brindle's way of tackling his column.

It would be a help because people are interested in things like that. And I know, of course, from the way he wrote, how highly he thought of you."

A dull red stain mottled the pitted face. "He was — he was like sunshine. You know that line: 'You came and the sun came after.' I don't know who wrote it but he always made me think of it. When he came into a room it — brightened." She struggled for expression, tried to speak, gave it up. After a moment she walked to the Dutch door so that her face was hidden from Lois. She said abruptly, "He made me feel attractive."

"What a wonderful thing — to go through life without making enemies," Lois said and heard Ethel draw in her breath sharply.

Something moved at the window and Joe Hattery, lifting a pane of glass, smirked. "The guy who could do no wrong," he said.

Ethel wheeled and went out of the cottage. As he used the putty knife Joe began to whistle.

Lois returned to the photograph album, grateful that the pictures were arranged chronologically. There was Roger at fifteen, already very big, towering over other boys. Roger and a small, scrawny looking lad who stared up at him with worship in his eyes. Underneath was written, "Roger and Albert." This must be Albert Kibbee. Roger at eighteen with a small, pale, bespectacled Albert. Roger graduating from high school, Roger on a bicycle, Roger with Albert again. Roger and a tall girl sitting on a fallen tree, laughing. Underneath was written, "My beloved Jane, the day she promised to marry me."

Lois lingered over that picture for a long time. Something of the relationship between those two surprised her. They were not touching each other but in their expression there was a completeness for which she had not been prepared. They belonged together, she thought. In some essential way they supplemented each other. What puzzled Lois was a sense of recognition, of familiarity, which faded little by little.

She began to turn the pages more rapidly. There were pictures of townspeople, later of men and women famous in their various fields, and always, of course, Roger and Albert, fewer of Jane, then none of Jane. And at last a picture of Roger in formal morning dress, smiling down with a kind of protective tenderness at Carol who was extremely lovely in trailing white satin and a filmy wedding veil. Under it, "My sweet little wife on our wedding day."

The pictures ended there. Lois closed the album and pushed it away, looking unseeingly at the wall above the table, thinking of the contrast between the magnetic look exchanged by Roger and Jane and his protective, amused tenderness for Carol. Not the usual story of a successful man discarding an aging wife for a pretty younger one. There was no rapture in this second marriage of his. Strange.

There was a tap on the door. "Come," she called without looking around. Joe Hattery set something down on the floor with a bang.

"Brought you an electric heater." His eyes slid over Lois, traveled around the room, rested on the couch, lingered on the hole in the frame.

"Thank you." Lois turned her back but Joe did not leave. He wandered across the room, absently lifted a cushion and let it drop again. Lois wished that he would go. She hated having him hover behind her like an evil bird.

"I guess," he said, "there's a lot of money in writing."

She made no comment.

"The first Mrs. Brindle's done well, hasn't she? Made a pot out of those articles."

"She's a fine writer," Lois replied, hoping that he would go.

"That's what I figured." She heard shoe leather creak as he shifted position. "Successful. Costs quite a bit to stay at the inn."

Lois pulled out the first volume of the scrap books and slammed it open. After a moment's indecision Joe went out and closed the door.

ii

Hours later, when she found herself straining to decipher the printed pages, Lois switched on the big desk lamp. She straightened up, the back of her neck aching, but still so absorbed that she was only dimly aware of her discomfort.

What a gift the man had had! After a somewhat fumbling beginning, in which he had imitated half a dozen columnists while he groped his way toward his own style and subject matter, he had handled his material with a vividness that impressed her by its cumulative effect. He had the rarest of abilities, that of communicating his own excitement, his own warm interest in daily life and the people around him. True, he had made them a little more than lifesize, endowed them with qualities they had not possessed. Albert the dreamer had had more than a touch of St. Francis; Bessie might have stepped out of Dickens; Ethel, faithful and devoted and helpful, bore no relation to the passionate, pockmarked woman who had hovered at the worktable; Joe, the unfortunate, was no reasonable facsimile of the insinuating bird of prey who had wanted to tell her something and had not dared. Carol, the child wife — oh, no, no!

And yet — she reached once more for the book of pictures and looked at the one which ended the book: Roger smiling down at his bride with protective tenderness. And yet he had believed what he had written. That was why his writing had carried such conviction. Until those past few months and, increasingly, the past few weeks. Then the writing was no longer easy, no longer exuberant. He had tried too hard, striving to recapture a magic that was gone. Somewhere he had lost what most of us lose in youth, the sense of wonder. He seemed constantly, with unutterable effort, to be attempting to reanimate himself. And he sounded tired.

The door opened and Bessie Kibbee came in carrying a big tray. Lois hastened to clear off the table.

"That's too heavy for you," she protested.

"Clyde took Paula for a drive and that Joe is never where you want him." Bessie removed covers and Lois saw lamb chops, creamed potatoes and peas, hot rolls and mint jelly, a tossed salad and lemon pie. There was also a frosty cocktail shaker.

"Shandy fixed it," Bessie explained. "Said you used to like bacardi cocktails. Know what? It's the first time Shandy has gone anywheres. He came over, all dressed up. It takes Jane Brindle to work miracles. If only Albert would see her —"

"She seems nice."

"Jane is just plain good," Bessie declared. "No one like her. But she's Albert's blind spot. I can't imagine what got into him. Yes, of course, I can too. It was Roger. And where Roger was concerned —"

She mopped her face. "You sit down and eat while it's hot. And drink your cocktail right away."

"There's too much for one person," Lois exclaimed. "Won't you join me?"

"I've got dinner to fix for Albert and Clyde and I've asked Paula Case to come. Carol's going out. But I'll sit a spell. No telling when the youngsters will get back." She sat down while Lois poured a cocktail and refused one for herself. "Albert can't hardly wait to talk to you. But there's one thing, Mrs. Fleming; Albert's a saint himself, you'll find that out soon enough, and he sees people in a kind of unworldly way. Roger was no angel, whatever they'll tell you around here. He was lusty. He liked women. Carol would scalp me for this, but he was nothing more than a chaser. He liked to drink, though he tried his best to keep people from finding out."

Sipping the ice-cold cocktail with its tang of lime, Lois blessed Shandy. Tired from her engrossing reading, her mind was at rest and did not follow Bessie closely, though she watched her with interested eyes, a trick she had learned in dealing with "authors" who had what she termed circular minds, which surrounded a point instead of going straight to it. She had learned not to interrupt, not to try to shift focus, not to hurry them; for often out of the rambling came invaluable information she could obtain only by indirection.

"Albert," Bessie went on, "is a dreamer. He creates things in his own image and believes they are true. He's just too idealistic for a practical world. Sometimes I think he'd have been better off if he'd spent as much time building himself up as he did Roger. Say what you like, Albert made Roger. I always thought so; I always will. But now it's time for the dead to bury their dead and for Albert to give some thought to the living. Right now I believe he's thinking more about Roger than he is about his own son. Of course, he hardly knows Clyde yet, and he — but it takes time to get to see anyone's good qualities, I always say. Clyde needs love; he needs to be important to someone. And the only girl around is Paula, who doesn't know he's alive. Girls who go chasing older men —

"Well, dinner still to get and Clyde will want some shirts ironed before tomorrow. Never a free moment." She nodded to Lois. "But I guess you're the same way. Conscientious. Know what? When I came in I was betting you'd be hard at work. Well, sometimes I think the clinging vine's better off but I don't know. We have to be what we are, I guess."

After dinner, Lois lighted a cigarette and went out onto Roger's walled terrace. She was so steeped in his work that his presence seemed to inhabit the place still, filling the big chair in front of the table, walking in this small cleared space, which he had had to fence in to obtain privacy. A friendly ghost but an uneasy one.

When the sun set the air became too chilly for comfort and she went indoors, pacing restlessly up and down the room. In time she discovered that she was really cold and slipped on a sweater. She felt oddly disturbed. Not about the work itself. There was ample material for four colorful articles. What disturbed her was the man who refused to stay dead, whose presence was so palpable in the room. She remembered how the impression of his head had remained in one of the down cushions when she first arrived. And the frame of the couch had a bullet hole in it.

That was what was bothering her then. Might as well take it out and look at it. Something was wrong here. Not just the bullet hole. After all, as Shandy had pointed out, no one had been shot. There were all kinds of innocent explanations for bullet holes. But none of them took into account Ethel Hattery smashing the windowpane or Shandy removing the bullet in that surreptitious way.

She plugged in the electric heater and in a few moments felt warm, more relaxed. But not at ease. She found herself fidgeting, moving uneasily. Something about the cottage made her nervous. Surely, she chided herself, she wasn't so superstitious that she feared the place because Roger Brindle had died there. It was the uncurtained windows that made her feel insecure, as they do most women. But no one was looking at her. Nerves, the doctor had said. Nerves. She needed a rest, that was all.

She glanced at her watch. I must go to bed, she told herself, but she made no effort to move. The windows were becoming an obsession. No one was outside. No one could be.

By an effort of will she forced her attention away from them. But someone had stood outside one of the windows recently and fired a bullet through the glass. Someone — she got up and went over to the couch. She found the hole near the top, a small hole that she could cover with her little finger, the hole that had so fascinated Joe Hattery a few hours earlier.

She stood in front of the couch, her hands thrust into the pockets of her sweater, lower lip caught between her teeth. Attempted murder? But Roger Brindle had not been shot. No one had been shot.

It didn't make sense. She took the cushions off the couch and found the mechanism that opened it into a bed. She undressed quickly, pulling over her head the chiffon nightgown Aunt Barbara had sent on her birthday. It fell over her head in a filmy cloud of accordion pleats. Indecent, she thought, but becoming. A gown like this is wasted on a widow. Damn those windows! A little more of this and I'll run screaming up the hill to Shandy.

She unplugged the electric heater, switched off the light, opened the window. And heard a dry twig snap.

Someone is watching me, she thought. She jumped back from the window, her heart thumping, groped her way to the front door and the Dutch door to make sure they were locked and climbed into bed, pulling the covers over her. A woods animal, an opossum perhaps, that was all it could be.

She turned on her side, trying to drive her uneasiness away by planning tomorrow's work. I must write Mignonne about Jane Brindle, she thought. I wonder why I wasn't told about her. What ended that wonderful marriage? Roger never loved Carol as he did Jane. Is it true that Carol is trying to drive her niece away from the house? What became of the woman Shandy planned to marry? Why does he distrust me? "Catching us unprepared," he said.

This was nonsense. She was going to forget the whole thing, put aside the night fancies which, she knew by experience, were unreliable. She was going to sleep.

Two hours later, still staring wakefully into the dark, she spoke aloud. "But it was gas I smelled!"

SEVEN

A knock on the door awakened her. Sunlight flooded the cottage which, the night before, had been filled with shadows and terror. Nothing could hide, threatening her, in this cheerful brightness. Lois slid her feet into mules and pulled on a tailored blue flannel robe. When she opened the door Clyde Kibbee was holding a tray covered by a linen napkin.

Being Clyde, he rushed into apology. "Mother didn't remember to ask what time you want breakfast. I didn't mean to wake you."

She yawned and then laughed and he laughed with her. With her face flushed by sleep and her curly hair standing up wildly she looked as young as he.

"What time is it?"

"A little after nine."

"I didn't sleep until quite late. There were — noises." And even in the bright warmth of morning she shivered, recalling her fear in the night. "Do you have prowlers around here?"

"Never," Clyde assured her.

Lois stood aside while he carried the tray to the table and removed the napkin and silver covers from toast and scrambled eggs and crisp bacon. There was a cool melon, a little jar of jam and a big pot of coffee.

Seeing her expression he smiled diffidently. "Mother loves to feed people and she thinks you are too thin. If you aren't firm with her you'll be getting oatmeal with thick cream."

"How kind she must be!"

The boy's eyes warmed. "She's pretty swell. I'll give her a testimonial any time. You'd better eat while it's hot."

He lingered while Lois poured her coffee and she realized that he was lonely, fearing to press his claim lest he be rejected.

"Do sit down and have some of this coffee with me," she urged him.

Obviously he wanted to but he shook his head, not quite believing he was welcome.

"You might be able to help me by telling me about these people."

He grinned apologetically. "I'm a stranger here myself. Haven't been around my folks since I was a little kid and hardly had my nose in Stoweville except for the funeral." He added slowly, "I didn't want to go. No reason I can see for making a fuss over a guy who was practically a stranger to me." Talking about himself increased his shyness. He backed to the door. "I must get back, but thank you, Mrs. Fleming. Father wants to meet you. He is stronger today. If you'd care to come down to the cottage some time this morning — by afternoon he is apt to be tired. He couldn't even see the first Mrs. Brindle yesterday. Only what tires him so much I don't know. He's not supposed to get out of bed."

"I'll come," Lois promised. "And I'll try not to tire him. Sling me out if I do." As Clyde started for the door she called, "And please tell your mother — no, I'll tell her myself. You'd never do justice to this breakfast."

When she had finished, and she ate more than she had expected, she dressed in a sleeveless white linen dress — I may be thin but I don't need falsies, she thought — and slung a powder blue sweater over her shoulders. As she reached the door there was a tap and she opened it to Jane Brindle, a very tailored Jane in dark green slacks, white blouse and flat walking shoes. She was taller by inches than Lois. She smiled and again Lois was aware of the charm of this plain woman.

"I thought," she began in her lovely voice and then noticed Lois's sweater. "Am I disturbing you? Were you going out?"

"Please come in. I've been hoping I'd have an opportunity to talk to you."

"Do you feel like a walk?"

"I'd love it."

When they were outside the cottage, Lois went around to the side. The ground here was rocky. Scattered among the boulders were a few hardy ribbon plants. The two directly below the window had been trampled. Lois bent over and saw that the damage had been done recently. When she looked into the cottage she was shocked to discover how clearly she could see. At night, with the lights on, there might as well not be any walls, she thought.

Who had stood here the night before, watching her? Stood for hours, because she had been aware of that unseen presence for a long time. Watched while she undressed and slipped a filmy nightgown over her head?

"What is it?" Jane Brindle asked at length.

Lois indicated the trampled ribbon plants. "Someone was watching me last night. I heard them. This morning I asked Clyde about prowlers but he says they never have any around here."

"Clyde," Jane said thoughtfully.

Together the two women strolled up into the scented freshness of the woods. Lois did not attempt to speak. For some reason Jane Brindle had sought her out and she was content to wait for the other woman to make the first move.

"I've just come from the Kibbees' cottage," Jane said. "Albert won't see me. And it's perfectly ridiculous when, for years and years, we saw each other almost every day."

Lois did not know what response to make to this and again she waited. Jane swung along at her side, deep bosomed, flat stomached, hands thrust into the pockets of her slacks. She seemed to be profoundly troubled.

At last she said with a little laugh, "You know, Albert has never forgiven me for divorcing Roger."

Lois strove for the same lightness. "What was it — a Damon-Pythias, Roland-Oliver friendship?"

"Not altogether. Not like that," Jane said slowly. "Albert saw Roger without faults, a perfect being. He attributed to him all the qualities he would have liked to have himself." Her walk had lost its easy rhythm, she was trudging heavily. "I've simply got to see him," she burst out. "Then I'll leave. I don't belong here. That's why I thought, if I could be of any help to you on the articles before I go — what can I tell you, Mrs. Fleming?"

Lois considered. "What was Roger Brindle like?"

Jane looked around, saw a fallen tree and sat down, pulling out of her pocket a package of cigarettes. When she did not speak Lois added, "What was his — goal in life?"

"You've been reading Adler," the older woman said with a quick smile. "A man's goal determines all his actions. Maybe. Roger's goal," she added thoughtfully, "was giving people what they wanted."

"A pretty big order," Lois commented.

"You know, Mrs. Fleming," Jane flicked ashes from her cigarette and clasped her arms around her knees, looking through the streaked sunlight on the leaves, "as a rule we expect so much more of others than we do of ourselves. We are impatient when they don't change their habits to suit us, but don't bother to change our own. All that. But Roger was the other way. He tried to make himself what others wanted him to be and he took them at their own valuation. Better than their own valuation. He simplified them because he was a very simple man, and he heightened their good qualities because he was essentially romantic."

Tears filled her eyes but she did not bother to wipe them away. "I'll love him till I die," she said simply. "He's in my bones." After a moment she went on, "There is a time in the life of most of us when we lose our sense of wonder, our expectation of adventure lurking behind the bend in the road, our belief in magic hiding behind a stone. Roger never lost that quality. He carried it with him always. He communicated a sense of heightened experience to those around him. The weather was never gray where he was.

"You have a big job, Mrs. Fleming; try, if you can, to make him real. He wanted so desperately to be real. And he blundered so disastrously. So disastrously." She put out her cigarette, taking her time.

It's coming now, Lois thought; what she really wants of me.

Jane stretched out her legs, staring at her sturdy boots. "Mignonne has spoken of you so often. She calls you a kind of divining rod, with a curious ability to get inside other people's skins, think with their minds, feel with their nerves. I don't know how you go at it, probably you don't know either. I write factual stuff myself. But try if you can to — find Roger."

But that wasn't what she had meant to say, Lois thought.

"He could have been a great man if he hadn't been so tragically weak." Jane straightened up briskly. "Well, I'll give you a rough outline, though you'll probably be able to get all that from other people. At least it will give you a kind of spine on which to construct your story."

Roger, she said, was left an orphan when he was only five years old; he had been brought up by relatives who never forgot they were doing their duty and never stopped talking about it. He had been, curiously enough, considering the man he later became, a shy child, so much bigger than other boys of his age that people expected, irrationally, that his mind and his emotions had grown with his body.

"You see, in a way, the pattern was set from the beginning. People expected too much of him." Jane leaned forward, resting her weight on her big, finely shaped hands, as though she read the story on the ground.

He had become a newspaper reporter; that was how they met, for Jane was working on the same paper. They had married with little to live on. And then Albert had lost his first church; he found he simply did not believe in it any longer, so Roger had taken care of him and Bessie.

"As a matter of fact, that's when Roger started *The Way I Heard It*. He needed extra money in order to support Albert. And the Kibbees had a baby right away. Well, Albert got other churches and lost them, and started a religion of his own and abandoned it, pursuing his dreams like bright balloons which always burst when he grasped them. But in the meantime Roger had hit his stride; he began to develop his own line. He became a popular success, more and more newspapers took the column, people quoted him, he was news."

Somewhere during those years they had been divorced; Jane passed over that without comment. And three years later Roger had married for the second time. His popularity mounted. And then, suddenly, without warning, he died.

"What a pity," Lois exclaimed, "for him to go at the very peak of his productive ability. I suppose his heart condition was the result of overwork."

"Nonsense! His heart was in perfect shape. I saw him a month before he died. Ran into him in a hotel lobby in New York and we had lunch together. He had just come to the city for a checkup and because he was — not sleeping."

"Oh! They told me he had died in his sleep. I just took it for granted that his heart had failed."

Lois's voice trailed off. Like lifting fog she became aware that this was the thing Jane had wanted to tell her. That Roger had not died of a heart attack. The whole confused picture fell into shape: Mignonne's evasiveness about the job; the jumbled dates of arrival, "catching us unprepared"; Jane Brindle's appearance after ten years. Divining rod. She wants me to find out how and why Roger died, Lois thought.

For a moment she was conscious only of her

94

fury at being hoaxed. At being used. Beside her, Jane was quiet, with a relaxation that required no twisting of hands, no movement of feet. Something in her was profoundly serene. I like her, Lois thought. I like her immensely.

"This is not for publication," Jane said; "simply to give you a sort of frame of reference. When I saw Roger a month ago he looked flushed, his eyes were bloodshot, his nose was getting a trifle bulbous, his mouth too lax."

"You mean he was drinking too much."

"Much too much. Being Roger, he was a secret drinker. He didn't want anyone to know that he was finding life too difficult to cope with. And, anyhow, he'd — rather recently he'd had a bad shock."

Lois groped her way cautiously. "Do you think — his second wife — ?"

"No, I don't," Jane said. "I don't believe Carol did him any harm. I'm not jealous. What Roger and I had no other woman could have touched. No, what I can't forgive Carol for is the ruthless thing she did to Shandy Stowe."

Carol, Lois thought. Carol. Of course, I should have seen that. Carol was the woman Shandy planned to marry. It has been implicit in everything she has said, in her proprietary manner.

Through a cloud she heard Jane saying, "Carol was his fiancée, but when he came back from the war, scarred and crippled, she jilted him and turned to Roger. And got him to buy Shandy's home for her into the bargain. When I had dinner with him last night and saw that he had become withdrawn and suspicious and bitter I could have slapped the woman cross-eyed. And the damnable part is that I believe he is still in love with her."

She stood up suddenly. "I'm keeping you. Albert Kibbee will be getting impatient. Try to persuade him to see me, will you, Mrs. Fleming? It would mean a great deal to me."

ii

Bessie Kibbee must have been on the lookout because she opened the door of the green cottage and slipped outside before Lois could knock.

"Albert's all keyed up," she said in a low voice, "but don't let him wear himself out. He wanted to get up and dress for you but I hid his clothes."

She led Lois through a shabby but meticulously neat living room and knocked on the bedroom door. After a moment a key turned in the lock and Albert Kibbee admitted them. Although Lois, under the stimulus of coffee and the sanity of sunlight, had sworn to rid herself of preconceptions and see these people as they were, Albert was the greatest disillusionment she had encountered.

He was a small man with a head too heavy for his scrawny neck, a fine forehead but a receding chin.

"Thank you for coming, Mrs. Fleming," he said in a reedy voice and she wondered why on

96

earth a man with such a voice had attempted to speak from a pulpit. When his wife had helped him back to bed and propped him high on pillows Lois took the chair that had been pulled up beside him.

"Ever since I heard about the biography of Roger," he began eagerly, "and that you were coming to work on it, I have wanted to talk to you. There is so much about him that no one else can tell you. I was his oldest friend and I knew him as no one else did."

His eyes held hers and Lois caught a glimpse of the man whom Roger had loved. They were a child's eyes, deep blue, clear as a phrase of Mozart. As he talked, Lois thought of Shandy's story of the man whose portrait had been done by so many artists. The picture Albert painted of Roger was in fresh, primary colors, as bright as those of Botticelli's Springtime, with the candid sweetness of a poem by George Herbert. Perhaps, after all, that was what Albert resembled, not St. Francis but George Herbert, last of the gentle saints to walk the earth. And through his words emerged the heart-warming story of a man who brought sunlight with him; a man who, in his thirst for affection and approval, had given both to others with a lavish hand.

Roger had been a lonely boy. Albert told her a story he had learned from one of his teachers. "She's an old lady now and runs the library here." Shortly after his mother's death, Roger had wandered, lost, through the garden of his parents' home. The teacher and some friends had been passing the house, talking of his mother's burial. The words had carried to the small child, who cried out, in anguish and denial, "No, no, not in the ground!" With his toy spade he had begun to dig frantically, furiously, hysterically, trying to find his lost mother.

"I remember my first meeting with him," Albert said, a tender smile curving his lips. "I was a little fellow, a runt without any physical courage, and Roger, even at fifteen, was six feet tall and powerful. He had the gentleness of a person so strong he never had to fight. I came on him in the woods. I wanted to climb a tree but I was afraid. So we did our homework together and then Roger helped me climb a tree to the topmost branch that would bear our weight. And I wasn't afraid at all because Roger was there."

He was silent for a long time, his eyes shining as he relived that moment when the wind had blown his hair and the branch had swayed and he had looked out over the world without fear. At length the radiance died out of his face and it was only a negative, faintly ridiculous little man who said matter of factly, "You know, Roger brought me and my wife together. I'd been fond of Bessie for a long time but I'd never have dared ask her to marry me if Roger hadn't encouraged me."

Dreamer? Lois asked herself. Fanatic? Idealist? What was Albert really? A perfectionist, at any rate. It must have been difficult for Roger Brindle to live up to such a picture. No wonder he had sounded so tired toward the end. So desperately tired. Tired enough to turn on the gas? she wondered.

The door opened and Clyde looked in. "Lunch is ready."

"Don't disturb me," Albert said sharply. "I want to talk to Mrs. Fleming without interruption."

Clyde withdrew, his sensitive face flaming.

"Sorry," Albert said. "That boy seems to have no consideration at all."

He spoke of his son as though he were a stranger, Lois thought, and then realized that Clyde had been away from home so much that he was almost as much of an outsider as she was herself. No wonder Bessie Kibbee had resented Roger and thought the time had come for Albert to give some of his devotion to his own boy.

"I forget — what were we talking about?"

In spite of his protests Lois got to her feet. "Another time. I promised not to tire you. Oh, by the way, Jane Brindle wants so much to see you."

"She had no right to come here. She forfeited that right." The little man sat erect, the muscles of his scrawny neck tight. "I'll never see her. Tell her that."

When the door had closed behind Lois she heard the key turn in the lock.

EIGHT

There was no one in sight when Lois passed the big house and went out between the heavy gate posts onto the country lane that led to the village. She walked slowly, enjoying the winding road, the arching trees, the momentary glimpses of the white spire of the village church, a red barn set in the midst of green fields, the curving line of hills, the glint of blue from a lake.

How lovely, she thought in delight, how peaceful. She stopped short, her breath cut off, as what appeared to be a heavy coil of rope uncoiled itself and slithered across the road. Her heart thumped. A snake in the garden of Eden.

Her bucolic mood was shattered and she came back to the problem that Jane Brindle had tacitly handed her. Nothing had been wrong with Roger's heart. How, then, had he died? At the core of the problem lay the fireplace and the odor of gas that had been trapped in the cottage which had been closed with what must have been panic haste after his death. Accident, suicide, murder? And what was she to do about it?

With a rueful grin she discovered that while her mind had been scurrying around in search of a solution, her subconscious had already made its decision. She was walking to the village in

100

search of Dr. Thomas, the family physician who had signed the death certificate, the genial "Doc" of Roger's column.

And yet why would anyone kill Roger? If it weren't for the bullet hole in the windowpane and the frame of the couch it could be accident or suicide. But though, as Shandy Stowe had reminded her, no one had been shot, the bullet hole meant intention. And who would kill America's best-loved man?

So strong, Carol had said; so weak, Jane had implied; so happy, so despairing. Like sunlight, Ethel Hattery had declared; a chaser of women, Bessie had stated bluntly, not attempting to conceal a smoldering dislike for the man who, by all accounts, had supported her and her husband all their married lives. So wonderful, Paula Case had said; nothing against him, Shandy had commented. What was Roger then? He gave people what they wanted. On that one point, at least, they had all agreed. But surely that was no motive for murder.

Unless, paradoxically, he had given too much. With three women apparently in love with him — his wife, his wife's niece, his secretary — the emotional temperature must have run high. And if women loved him, the men who loved the women must have hated him. Bessie had spoken bitterly of Paula chasing older men and giving no attention to Clyde; Joe Hattery had obviously been hostile to him; and Shandy — Shandy who, Jane believed, still loved Carol —

How incredible, Lois thought, to be looking at people as potential murderers. How fantastic. Well, I'll talk to Dr. Thomas and settle it once for all.

By the time she reached the village she was uncomfortably warm. The early morning chill was gone and the sun blazed down uncompromisingly. She walked slowly around the village green. In front of a small white house, freshly painted, with flower beds arranged for self-conscious prettiness, she found the neat plaque, Marshall Thomas, M.D.

She knocked at the door and a motherly looking woman with a beaming face admitted her.

"May I see the doctor?"

"He's out on a house call but he'll be back at any minute." The woman opened the door of a room that originally had been a parlor and now was a doctor's waiting room. The furniture was heavy, old-fashioned. It was typical, Lois thought, of the old-time family doctor's waiting room. She wondered vaguely why she was surprised and then realized that so few things conform to type. This atmosphere had deliberately been created. She recalled Bessie's caustic comment, "He'd so busy trying to be the old family doctor Roger made him out to be —"

"Will you be comfortable?" the woman asked. "I'm Doc's wife, Helen Thomas. Do let me give you a glass of lemonade. I just made some." She bustled out, not waiting for a reply.

Lois stood looking out on the green. How curi-

102

ous, she thought, that everyone seemed to be wearing himself out trying to be someone else. Mrs. Thomas was back almost at once with a frosty glass of lemonade. She settled herself comfortably in an old rocker.

"You're Mrs. Fleming, aren't you?" She laughed when she saw Lois's surprise. "Carol Brindle had supper — dinner, she calls it — with us last night. First time the poor girl's been anywhere since her great sorrow." Lois looked up quickly but Mrs. Thomas's face was bland as she employed Carol's own phrase. "She told us about you so I recognized you the minute you came up the steps. Short dark curly hair, she said; though she kind of forgot to say you're pretty." This time the hostility crept through. "She wanted Doc to help you any way he can. He'll be delighted."

"That's nice of him."

"Doc's only human. He can't say no to Carol any more than any other man can." She added without transition, "I hear the first Mrs. Brindle is back."

Lois made no comment. She was busy lighting a cigarette and trying to make herself secure on the slippery horsehair upholstery.

"One thing Carol couldn't be first in. She got Roger second hand." When Lois made no reply Mrs. Thomas tried again. "I hear Shandy Stowe took Jane Brindle to dinner last night. I always used to say, 'If there's something to be done, leave it to Jane.' "

103

She's trying to tell me something, Lois thought. How much does she know?

"That's quite a household for Carol to keep up," Mrs. Thomas remarked. "All Roger's waifs and strays: the Kibbees, the Hatterys, Paula Case."

"I thought Paula was Mrs. Brindle's niece."

"Well, yes, but it was Roger's idea to bring her to the house when her parents died. He was the one to keep her there. I always say a married woman is asking for trouble when she brings a younger woman into her house. Not that Paula is any match for her aunt when it comes to looks, but seventeen — there's a lot of appeal just in being seventeen."

Lois felt her way. "She seems to be rather a nervous child."

"Nervous! When Roger died, Doc had more trouble with the niece and the secretary than he did with Carol, I can tell you. Paula cried her eyes out and Ethel Hattery went right straight into hysterics. He had to give her a hypodermic to quiet her." She added, "Of course, Roger was the virile type —" she let the sentence fall. To her disappointment Lois did not pick it up.

"Not that Carol didn't act heartbroken," Mrs. Thomas tried again. "Only she didn't seem so — surprised, somehow." Her voice dwindled off and then she started on another tack. "Pity you weren't here for the funeral. People came from everywhere. Even brought out the Kibbee boy. First time I'd laid eyes on him." She added thoughtfully, "Gave me quite a shock."

A car stopped outside the house and Mrs. Thomas heaved herself out of the rocker to go to the window. "There's Doc now. I'll just tell him you're here." She went out and absentmindedly closed the door of the waiting room behind her. Lois heard sibilant whispering in the hall, the door opened and Doc came in. Really, Lois thought, this is absurd. No country doctor ever looked as much like one as Dr. Thomas. He was short and plump and calculatedly untidy, with a big booming laugh and a hearty bedside manner.

"Well, Mrs. Fleming, glad to see you. Helen told me you were here. What can Doc do for you? Carol said you'd be around to get some stories about Roger. Well, you've come to the right man."

The telephone rang and he answered it with the heartiness that was beginning to oppress Lois. "Hello, there. Doc Thomas speaking. . . . Well, now, I declare, that's too bad. . . . Abdominal pains? . . . Uh huh. Well, now, nothing to worry about. Nosirree. You just bundle her into bed and give her a big dose of castor oil. And tell her those are Doc's orders and no back talk."

Castor oil for abdominal pains, Lois thought, appalled.

He put down the phone and beamed at her. Beaming, she decided, was what the Thomases did best. "One of my little patients. Brought that kid into the world."

And at this rate you'll soon send her out of

it, Lois answered him mentally.

"Well, now, let's see what Doc can do for you." He fitted his hands neatly together and peered down over his spectacles. "Roger Brindle. If you read his column — and who didn't? — you know he and I were —" (Oh, no, don't say it, Lois protested in her mind) — "buddies," he finished inevitably. "Ever see him?"

"Only photographs."

"Big guy, six-four, with a face like those carved on mountains. Rugged, you know. Everyone liked Roger. He had a kind of exuberance. A party always picked up when he came in. Tremendous vitality." He pondered for a moment. "You know, it's queer," he said in a tone of surprise, "it's kind of hard to quote him, to tell you things he said. Without his voice and his ways they don't sound like much. I don't know what there was about him —"

"It's hard to define the things that make personality," Lois agreed.

"I guess that's it. Well, I met him when he first came to Stoweville to be a reporter. He and his first wife were both working on the paper here. Understand Jane's come back."

Lois nodded.

"Smart newspaper woman," he said. "Very nice person, if you know what I mean. Don't know what broke up that marriage. Roger never talked about it. Did him a lot of damage at the time but after he married Carol he was all right again. Gorgeous creature, Carol."

"She's a very pretty woman," Lois agreed.

"And Roger made a lot of her. Bought the Stowe house and gave her every single thing her heart desired. The Cases were poor as church mice but she's had it nice ever since she married. Don't know what the poor girl will do now. I'd have thought Roger would leave something. He was so successful." He made a juicy, mouth-filling word of successful, letting it linger on his palate, savoring it.

"Perhaps," Lois suggested carefully, "he thought he had plenty of time to make arrangements for her. He thought he was in good health."

Dr. Thomas gave her a quick look. "That old pump of his — I'd been warning him about that. Guess I was the only one who wasn't surprised when it stopped on him."

"How odd! I understood from the first Mrs. Brindle that a New York specialist gave him a clean bill of health only a month before he died."

Doc stopped beaming; he watched Lois steadily. He knows Roger's heart was sound but he won't tell me the truth, she thought. He can't afford to; he's the infallible old Doc. He'll never admit he made a mistake. And it's more than a mistake. If I could smell gas ten days after Roger died —

"The best of specialists can be wrong," he said. "There have been a lot of cases. They tell a man he's all right and he walks out of the consulting room and falls dead on the street." He added casually, "I didn't know Roger had seen Jane since the divorce."

"They ran across each other by accident in New York. Mrs. Brindle thought," Lois added, "he looked depressed."

Doc rubbed his hand over his chin. "Too bad," he said sadly, "for her to come back and stir things up. Dog-in-the-manger stuff, as though Roger couldn't be happy with anyone but her. He was the least depressed man I ever knew." He looked ostentatiously at his watch. "Well, Mrs. Fleming, I'm mighty glad you dropped in. I'll try to think up some stories about Roger for those articles." He scraped back his chair. "He wrote about me to the point," he said heartily, "where so many people knew me by name that it might make the stories better to say I told 'em."

"Oh, of course," Lois agreed. With this approach she was completely at home.

He took her hand in his and patted it. The beam was working once more. "Don't let anyone give you any — funny ideas about Roger. We want those articles to be the kind he'd be proud of, don't we? Sure?" He patted her hand again and Lois wondered wildly if he would offer her a lollypop. "And the kind Carol can sign with a clear conscience. Sure we do. There's always a lot of gossip about a man as famous as Roger. But you know that yourself. You've come across the troublemakers before. You'll hear things about why he kept the Hatterys around. But don't you pay any attention. Ethel was a fine secretary and he was mighty nice to her husband, considering what Joe is. You want to be cautious about listening to anything Joe has to say. Criminal, you know." He shook his head. "But that was Roger. Too kind for his own good."

He led her to the outer door. "Helen and I want you to come to supper some night. She'll call you. 'Bye now."

Well, Lois thought as she walked away from the house, conscious that Doc, in full view of the green, was beaming after her retreating figure, well, that's that. The man is lying his head off. Roger Brindle was killed and I can't pretend it isn't so. But what should I do? If I go to the police they'll laugh at me. Dr. Thomas is well known; they'll take his word. It would be easy to accept that, to tell myself I can't do anything on my own and anyhow it doesn't concern me. Only, she admitted, you can't live like that. This was going to be unpleasant but she had to go ahead.

What now? She saw a clock on the town hall. Two-thirty. Across the street was a chain grocery store with a succession of vehicles turning in to its spacious parking lot at the back: shining station wagons, Cadillacs, a Model T Ford. A few farmers walked down the street and women in housedresses, women in slacks, women in blue jeans, women in shorts. The fewer clothes, the surer one was that they were New Yorkers. The natives kept their clothes on. There was a gift shop, which also had a lending library and sold bus tickets; a post office, an ivy-covered red-brick house that had been turned into a library. Lois turned abruptly and went up the steps.

The library was cooler than the street and quiet, the silence broken only by the gasping whir of an electric fan that needed oil. On either side of the entrance were rooms lined with books so badly lighted that it was difficult to decipher the titles. At a center table in the room to the left sat an elderly woman.

Lois went up to the table and the woman looked up at her.

"I am Lois Fleming. Mr. Kibbee was telling me about you this morning. He said you'd been his teacher when he was a boy."

The librarian smiled. "His and Roger Brindle's. They were in the same class. Remember it as if it was yesterday. Better than if it was yesterday. Albert always was a little runt and he was pint-sized then; and Roger just towered over the class. But Albert was the brains, he was the smart one. In a way, that is. He'd have been smarter, of course, to see Roger wasn't real."

Lois snapped to attention. This woman had seen the intangible quality which Jane Brindle had mentioned. The librarian observed Lois's expression and her own was shrewd.

"David and Goliath," she said unexpectedly. "You're no fool. Nice type. You can get people talking but you're not taken in. That's the thing. Not to be taken in. You've got to watch that when people start telling you about Roger. He had this town hypnotized; of course, he was the only celebrity who'd settled here since 1803 so people made a lot of him.

"There are some who'll tell you what a good friend Roger was, just so you'll know they knew him. People who like to touch the fringes of a famous person as though some of the fame would rub off on them. But the ones to look out for, if you want the truth, are those who really believed in him. Take Albert Kibbee, for instance." She shook her head. "Roger wasn't a man to Albert, he was a cult. Bessie Kibbee had no reason to love Roger, even if he did support them. Always in second place. Not like Carol who has to be first, regardless. And as for Clyde — of all the neglected children! If he resented Roger I'm the one who would never blame him, especially as I hear that he's fallen for Carol's little niece and —"

She stopped to tell a schoolboy where he would find books on aeronautics and turned back to Lois as though there had been no interruption. "But then I sized Roger up a long time ago. I can remember as if it was yesterday when his mother died; got thrown off a horse when she was riding with another man. Her husband, who was a poor stick anyhow, shot himself. So the boy was left an orphan with some strait-laced relatives. What was their name now? I had it right on the tip of my tongue."

"Mr. Kibbee," Lois said, "told me about Roger digging for his mother."

There was malice in the librarian's eyes. "Yes, he dug. That's when I began to get wise to Roger.

A little show-off he was. You see, I was passing when it happened — at least, the first time. And I guess it was genuine then. Only the girls with me were so touched and made such a fuss over the little fellow, kissing him and petting him and sympathizing with him, that he knew it paid. From then on, believe it or not, every time anyone went past the house he began to pull the same trick. He was a right surprised youngster when it stopped working and that aunt or cousin who took him over — what *was* her name? Know it as well as I do my own — paddled the seat of his pants for him."

She laughed. "Yes, that's Roger for you. Struck up a great friendship with Albert. Like everyone else, Albert was blind where Roger was concerned. To him Roger was everything he wanted to be. And Roger played on it. Took Albert fishing and birdnesting, but Albert did all his lessons for him. Always the same answers on their papers and the same mistakes. Albert was bright as a button but Roger was slow for his age. And, as I said, always a show-off. Needed admiration all the time and didn't care how he got it. Jane cleared out in good time, if you ask me. Everyone in town knows he's been sleeping with that secretary. Except Carol."

A look of surprise crossed her face. "You know, it never occurred to me before. Of course, Carol knew it too. That's the kind of thing a woman's friends never keep from her. Especially when the wife's pretty and the mistress looks like the Hattery woman, disfigured and dreary besides. It makes a fool of the wife. It just shows, if Roger would take up with Ethel he'd take up with anyone."

She reached for a palm leaf fan which rattled as she waved it back and forth. "Well, I suppose it served her right. Carol, I mean. Throwing over Shandy Stowe the way she did because he got his face all mangled up, and turning to Roger. Shandy shut himself up after that. Yes, I guess Carol got what was coming to her, what with Ethel Hattery and her own niece — I'll bet she makes life rough for Paula now. Carol always had to be first. I wouldn't like to be in that kid's shoes."

A couple of schoolgirls came in and handed her some books. She stamped them and the girls moved away toward the shelves. Apparently they intended to stay. Lois turned to leave.

"Guess you run across some odd stories," the librarian said. "Must be hard to get at the truth. People are so unreliable — Alice, I've told you before those medical books are for adults only. And tell your mother I'm holding a copy of the new Cronin novel for her."

NINE

A scant quarter mile beyond the dream village of Washington in Connecticut lies the Mayflower Inn, which had the remarkably good judgment not to create a foreign atmosphere and the good sense to discover that beauty, dignity, and vast crackling open fires provide a better welcome than the most astute maître d'hôtel trained in a Swiss hostelry.

After dinner Shandy led Lois out on the deep veranda. The stillness was broken only by the rustle of leaves, the chatter of a brook tumbling over pebbles at the foot of a ravine, the sleepy conversation of birds. Twilight lingered, revealing the line of rolling hills.

They smoked in silence that was without restraint, without any uneasy compulsion for speech.

"Last night, when I took Jane to dinner," Shandy said at length, "it was the first time in years I had gone to a public place. You've done that for me."

"I?" Lois asked in honest surprise.

"For some reason," Shandy tried to speak casually, "I was under the impression that I was — offensively scarred. I didn't want to put people off their feed in restaurants or anything like that.

I still have a tendency to shy away when someone takes a good look at me but the worst is over. The hard thing was making the start."

Lois was choked with rage and pity, neither of which would serve the purpose. "I'm glad it's over," she said inadequately.

Shandy laughed. "I like to see you lose your temper. I know you so well. You're perfectly furious, aren't you?"

"It was such a waste! All those years that you've withdrawn into yourself. Perhaps it would have been better for you, Shandy, if you hadn't been so filthy rich. You'd have had to get out on your own and you'd have discovered sooner that you weren't —"

"Horrible?" he prompted.

This time her anger flared. "Horrible? You were never, never like that. Scarred, yes, but nothing — repulsive, nothing to put people off their feed. Even when I knew you, when they were fresh and at their worst, any fool could see the scars didn't matter, that you were an unusually good-looking man. If anyone told you —" she broke off.

The trees had lost their color now and melted into the growing pattern of darkness; only the sky was still light. Shandy's hand reached for hers and closed over it, tightened until he hurt her, until it seemed that he would crush the bones.

"Why did you wait so long?" he asked harshly. "Why didn't you come sooner?"

The bitterness in his voice alarmed her. How

deep had the neurosis gone? And how responsible had his mutilated face been for the change in him? Was it Carol who had told him that he was repulsive, that he sickened her? Why had he abandoned his house to her? And why, more than all else, had he stayed so near her? Had Carol's attitude toward him changed when the scars faded, when she grew weary of being married to a man so much older than she? Had Shandy — and Lois knew that this question had been in her mind from the beginning — had he fired a shot at Roger Brindle? If not, why had he taken away the bullet?

Instinctively she tugged at her hand until he released it with a laugh that held a hint of mockery. But the mockery was directed at himself and made her ashamed of her own withdrawal. For some reason she could not be natural with Shandy and the knowledge disturbed her. He was charming; he was, in a sense, tragic. The truth was that she did not know the man he had become.

"What are you going to do now, Shandy? Surely you won't continue to live like a hermit."

"I don't know," he said flatly.

"But haven't you any interests?"

"I have one," he said provocatively. "Would you like to hear about it?"

He wants to sidetrack me, she thought; he is trying to bring back the past, a moment that's over, that's dead.

"Isn't anything in life worth doing?" she asked impatiently.

Shandy's voice was impersonal when he spoke again. "There's the village. Stoweville. I'd like to see the town meetings go back to the old tradition. Today it's mostly the professional politicians who are talking. I'd like to see the people on their feet, speaking their minds. You know, Lois, something has gone terribly wrong. For the first time in their history Americans are afraid to speak their minds. Afraid to disagree. Afraid to have an independent opinion. They conform to a line. Is the open mind suspect? If it is, we're through. Even if it's only in a village like Stoweville, I'd like to see them dare to speak their piece and stand by it."

"Then why don't you do something?" she demanded. When he made no reply she said, "Your old excuse is gone. It never was much good but now it's gone."

There was a longer silence this time. Once Shandy reached tentatively for her hand and then drew back his own. She heard him take a long breath.

"It's too late," he said at last. "If I were to attempt anything public — no, I don't mean the scars — there would be trouble. And now," in a tone of decision, "no more about me. You can't imagine how deathly sick I am of Shandy Stowe. Tell me about Lois Fleming, and explain, if you can, why the most vivid woman I know became a ghost."

Lois disregarded his comment. "Shandy, I've been thinking a lot about your story of the man

117

who was painted and sculpted by so many artists. I've been getting the most conflicting pictures of Roger Brindle; he was strong, he was weak; he was romantic, he was lusty; he was loved, he was hated."

"Jane said she would give you any help she could. She is really a magnificent woman. But why did she come back here, do you know?"

She wants to discover how Roger Brindle died, Lois thought. Aloud she said, "I don't know except that she'd like to see Mr. Kibbee and he won't have anything to do with her."

"Poor Albert." Shandy was amused. "The one-track mind. And yet there's a terrific strength in a man like that, Lois. His faith has a granite quality though I must admit it's tough on Bessie. She adores him, you know; she has even sacrificed her son to make her husband's life tranquil. She sits back, day after day, watching him burn incense on the altar of his god. There must have been times when she'd have liked to kill Roger."

The silence seemed to bother him. He got up. "You are cold. We had better start back."

He turned on the heater in the car, the head-lights flared and the car rolled out of the circular parking space and down the narrow road that led away from the inn. They had nearly reached New Milford when Shandy spoke out of the darkness.

"I love Jane," he said, "but I wish to God she'd go away."

"Are you afraid she'll stir things up?"

Shandy's head turned as he tried for a brief moment to read her face, shadowy in the darkness. He looked back at the road. "Why do you say that?"

"Because that's what Dr. Thomas warned me not to do."

"Oh."

She waited but he made no attempt to amplify the monosyllable.

"Shandy!" she exclaimed, resisting an impulse to stop the car, to shake words out of the man who was so determinedly taciturn.

"What is it?"

"How long are we going on like this, crawling around in that great pit of silence?"

"You sound annoyed."

"Don't be sarcastic. But this is preposterous. Why can't we discuss the situation honestly? I'm not just trying to stir things up."

"In other words," he said, "with zeal and good intentions you are hell-bent on knowing what happened to Roger Brindle."

"Why did you take away the bullet?"

It seemed to her that Shandy's tension relaxed, as though she had not asked the question he anticipated, the question he feared. It was the wrong question.

"Because," he said coolly, "I think that bullet was fired from my .22. Anyhow, that was a .22 bullet and I had a little .22 I carried in the car for awhile when there was a rash of hold-ups on the highways. Never used the thing. The war made me fed up with any kind of weapon. Anyhow, the thing is missing."

"But —"

"I don't know who. I don't know why, though I can guess about that. In fact, if I was pinned down — and don't try to do it — I could guess who. It happened two nights before Roger died. Someone stood outside the window and fired a shot at Roger who was, presumably, on the couch. No one was hurt. That's the story in a nutshell."

"But hasn't anyone —"

"No one has done anything; no one has said anything. The pane might have been broken by a stone or hail for any comment I've heard. As for Roger, he sealed over the hole in the pane and left it there."

"Why?"

Shandy shrugged. "Perhaps to remind someone that it was a near miss. Perhaps to remind himself to watch his step. Who knows? Odd, isn't it?"

He's lying, Lois thought. He's lying.

Shandy took the secondary road that led to Stoweville. He was driving faster now, although the road was hilly with a number of blind curves. He took one without slowing down and Lois was flung against him. Ridiculous, she told herself; it's just chemistry. I'm not a woman to be thrown into a flutter by a man's proximity. She drew as far away as she could.

He slowed down for Stoweville, swerved onto the road that led out of the village to the house that had been his. Outside the gates he stopped the car and turned to her.

"What," he asked politely, "do you intend to do?"

"Roger Brindle was murdered, wasn't he?"

"He was murdered." Shandy's pleasant voice was almost casual.

I'm not really shocked, Lois thought; I'm not genuinely surprised. It had to be that way. Only murder — it's something in the papers, it's a radio program. Murder doesn't strike at home. And Roger — Roger the well beloved, Roger surrounded by people who were objects of his kindness, Roger whom someone hated enough to kill.

"I asked you before: what do you intend to do? Stick to your job and write the articles like a good girl, tell the story of the life and times of America's peerless man, or stir up the animals?"

"We have no right to keep still about murder."

"Suppose you interfere," Shandy pointed out reasonably, "do you realize what will happen? You'll be regarded as a meddlesome female with a bee in her bonnet. You'd be laughed at. And the people who admire Roger Brindle will crucify you for starting a scandal about him. Doc Thomas issued the death certificate. He'll lie himself black in the face. In fact, he has lied himself black in the face. As soon as Roger was found, his body was carried up to his own room in the house and the cottage closed up. If you hadn't come so soon it would have been cleared of every evidence of his death before your arrival."

"Do you mean that everyone here is living in a kind of conspiracy of silence?"

Shandy said nothing.

"But who could buy silence like that?"

Shandy did not move, his hands still rested lightly on the wheel, but Lois found herself fumbling for the catch on the door. He started the car and drove into the garage.

"Better wait for me," he said as she got out. "You'll never be able to find your way without a flashlight. You don't want to — get hurt."

She waited in the darkness. The motor raced for a moment, was shut off, she heard Shandy's somewhat halting gait in the garage, the door was rolled down, and then he was beside her, his flashlight casting a beam on the ground.

Lois looked up at the dark house and it seemed to her that something moved at one of the windows. Probably just a curtain blowing in the wind, she thought. But there was no wind. They did not speak until they were out of range of the house, moving up the hill into the woods.

"Nervous here?" Shandy asked, again with the politeness that made her a stranger.

"Someone was watching me last night. I didn't like it."

"Sure? Not just country noises?"

"I'm sure. Someone was outside the window most of the evening and while I undressed."

"That won't happen again," he promised grimly.

"Why do you say that? Do you know who it was?"

"Probably Joe Hattery. Unsavory little beast. He's building himself up quite a score."

He opened the door of the cottage for her.

"You didn't lock it?"

"I never thought. Here in the country it seems unnecessary."

"I think," Shandy advised her, "I'd lock it after this. No use —" He stepped in after her.

Lois turned quickly, in a panic. "Good night, Shandy. Thanks for dinner."

"I won't stay," he answered her unspoken comment. "You needn't be so alarmed."

"Stop acting like a fool, can't you?" she said in exasperation.

He laughed softly. "You can't have it both ways. You'll have to figure out just what you think of me. All I want is to look around and make sure everything is —" His hand was on the light switch. He let it drop, turned off his flashlight, moved forward.

"What —"

"Quiet." His voice was hardly more than a breath. "Someone in the patio. Saw a light. No, stay here." She heard him cross the room, heard him fumble with the bolt on the Dutch door.

In spite of his injunction she followed him, groping her way across the room. Her hand brushed his arm, closed around it. She peered over his shoulder. A flashlight made a path in the patio, brushed the trunk of the big elm tree.

She gripped his arm tighter, struck an ornament on the table and knocked it to the floor. In the patio the flashlight was switched off.

Shandy was moving forward and Lois's hand tightened on his arm.

"Stay here," she whispered. "He may be armed."

The intruder was running now. The gate in the fence creaked as he opened it and then clanged shut. Shandy switched on his flashlight, and he swore as he felt in his pockets.

"What's wrong?" she asked.

"That lock is automatic and I left my key at home."

Lois brought him hers and he ran through the patio, unlocked the gate. She saw the flashlight moving in a wide arc as he swept the woods. And then someone was breathing beside her, labored, rapid breathing. But there was no other sound. She stood stock still, afraid to release her own breath, to make a movement. There was only the darkness and the heavy breathing, so terribly near her. Then the faint sound of cloth brushing against cloth. The intruder was moving away from her, toward the open front door. Even in the midst of her panic, her mind followed that almost noiseless withdrawal. How well he knew the cottage, to be able to cross the room in the dark without blundering into the furniture.

And then the cottage was empty. The labored breathing was gone. Lois let out her pent-up breath in a gasp and filled her lungs deeply. She was shivering.

The gate in the fence creaked again and Shandy's torch threw an arc of light across the terrace.

"Well," he said when he returned, "I guess that's that."

"Shandy!" She clutched at him with both hands.

"You're shaking." He drew her into his arms. "Nothing to worry about. Whoever it was got away."

"He just slammed the gate," she told him. "He doubled back and came through here. I could have touched him. He's someone who knows the cottage well, Shandy."

His arms tightened. "You can't be sure of that."

"But he knew his way in the dark."

"Lois." There was a warning in Shandy's voice. When she made no reply he shook her lightly, his hands gripping her shoulders. "Listen to me! Roger never let outsiders come to the cottage. He worked here and he refused to be disturbed. Do you understand?"

"Yes," she said. "It was someone who lived here."

His hands dropped. "I'll have a new lock put on for you tomorrow. Better prop chairs under the doorknobs tonight. You can set the telephone on the floor right beside the couch. My number is 211 and ring three times."

He switched on the lights and stood looking down at her. Without warning he gathered her into his arms, tipped back her head, bent over her. Then he laughed, kissed her cheek lightly and went out.

TEN

Carol Brindle lay on the couch in the library, wearing a filmy gray dress like a cloud, her tawny hair bright in the sunshine that touched her golden arms. She was, Lois thought, almost a beautiful woman. The trouble was that you could not get at her; it was hard to tell whether she was clever or whether there was simply nothing to find behind that languorous exterior.

When she turned from Roger's widow to his secretary, Lois was aware of a shock. Ethel sat bent over the open notebook on her lap. The flaxen braids were as severe as ever. The sun was cruel to the pockmarked face. As usual her stockings were twisted, her shoes were run down at the heels, her cotton dress looked as though she had put it on without pressing it.

"He made me feel attractive," she had said of Roger Brindle.

Unless one had a deeper awareness than one was ever likely to have of another person's inner needs, it was always difficult to account for the mutual attraction between outwardly incompatible people. Ethel was not only infinitely less attractive than Carol, she was essentially dreary, without the leaven of humor, without a scrap of charm. What could have possessed the man?

Lois found her eyes resting speculatively on Ethel. If it had been Joe Hattery prowling on the terrace the night before, Joe who had looked in her window, did Ethel know of his activities? She must know if her husband left the cottage at night. Perhaps, by dropping a hint, it would be possible to stop him. Peeping Tom or something worse?

Lois brought her mind back to the job at hand. The notes for the article were not advancing. Carol was perfectly willing to talk but it was obvious that she wanted the story to deal primarily with her marriage to Roger, with his devotion to her.

"You met him in 1946," Lois prodded.

"Oh, I'd met him before that at a meeting of some kind right after I moved to Stoweville. He was making a speech and everyone turned out for it. And then, of course, the whole village knew him, more or less. I mean, we spoke on the street and all that. But it was in 1946 that we really got acquainted. Of course, I was engaged to be married to another man then."

With a lazy movement Carol turned so that the eyes which were so nearly yellow met Lois's. "I was going to marry Shandy Stowe — until he came back from the war like that. Then he didn't think it was fair to me. But I guess he's never really gotten over it, poor darling. He was terribly generous; he knew I loved this house and he sold it to Roger, but he always stayed near by. I don't mean there was anything — wrong. Devotion like that is pretty rare, I can tell you. Shandy deserves — well, of course, in my great sorrow — but in time — after all, I'm still young and Roger wouldn't want me to grieve for him forever."

Ethel Hattery wrote stolidly. Carol still smiled at Lois. She saw us come in last night, Lois thought; she was at the window, watching. She is staking her claim to Shandy.

In spite of her effort to appear unconscious of Carol's maneuver, Lois found that her voice was too crisp, too artificially impersonal as she went on, "So you really became friends with Mr. Brindle in 1946?"

Carol nodded. "You can imagine how thrilled I was. Of course, he wasn't rich like Shandy but he was more important. I mean, everyone knew him, not just in Stoweville but in New York and all over the country. It was wonderful to go any-where with him. When he walked in —"

"The long-awaited guest." Ethel's interruption was unexpected.

"No," Carol said literally, "he was hardly ever late. Well, anyhow, he bought this house and we came here after our honeymoon. And we were so happy; Roger just seemed to spend all his time trying to find out what I'd like. He spoiled me, I guess. I wouldn't want you to say anything about his first wife; she's all right in her way, I suppose; but you could make it clear he never loved anyone but me, though women just wouldn't let him alone."

A dull red mottled Ethel Hattery's face. Lois

saw a pulse beating in her throat, saw her fingers tremble as she grasped the pencil.

Carol stretched her arms over her head. It seemed to Lois that she could almost hear her purring. "Roger was a moderate man in everything," she continued. "He smoked very little, rarely took a drink. Of course, he did too much. People took advantage of his kindness. They made so many demands on him. He even — I know Ethel won't mind my telling you — he took her husband when he got out of prison and gave him a job here. He was very — charitable"

The baiting of Ethel was beginning to make Lois acutely uncomfortable. She searched for a topic that would have the safety of impersonality.

"You know," Carol went on with apparent irrelevance, "I simply can't believe it's as hard for people to get jobs as they say. Albert, of course, is different; he's an eccentric, and anyhow Bessie earns their keep by doing the cooking and housework here."

Considering the size of the house, Lois thought indignantly, I should think so. I wonder if Carol knows she has been exploiting that woman, or whether she cares. If Roger was so all-fired kind, why did he allow anything so outrageous?

"But," Carol persisted in her soft voice, "there should be something Paula can do to support herself. Wouldn't you think so, Mrs. Fleming? A girl of that age is too much responsibility for me. And so sullen. You can hardly get a word out of her."

She looked up to see Paula standing in the door-way. At sight of the girl the three women sat transfixed. She was holding a revolver in her hand. Then she came forward slowly and thrust it at Carol.

"I just found this," she said. There was fear in her face but there was defiance too.

Carol jumped to her feet, moving away from the girl. "Are you crazy?" she screamed. "Take that thing away at once. It might be loaded."

"It's yours, isn't it?"

"Mine? Don't be ridiculous. I never saw the thing before."

Paula dropped it on the carpet. "What a liar you are," she said contemptuously.

With a deep sigh Ethel Hattery pitched out of her chair in a faint.

ii

After the emotions in the big house, Albert's bedroom in the Kibbee cottage seemed as cool, as serene as a cloister. His eyes, deep and blue and mystical, rested tranquilly on Lois.

"I can talk to you," he said. "There are so few people I can talk to. Roger was one of them, almost the only one. He understood. Not just the tangible things but the intangible. 'I lived with visions for my company.' Bessie," his smile was rueful, "doesn't think visions are practical. But they are good company. And always there's

130

the possibility, however remote it may be, that they will become real. In fact, if you believe hard enough, they do become real."

He seemed as unsubstantial as a cloud, and so frankly happy to be talking to her that Lois found herself feeling a kind of fondness for the little man.

"Tell me about your search for a church," she suggested.

His clear eyes clouded. "They compromised. Each time I would think: Surely this is the way to worship God, to find Him. But after awhile someone would come to me and say, 'You must be careful about what you preach. Don't condemn this so completely. Soft-pedal that. After all, one can't expect too much of people. We're only human. You are turning the congregation against you.' And then I'd know it was only lip service again. Just lip service. But if God is perfect He must be worshiped perfectly. We shouldn't be satisfied with less than perfection."

Lois felt an ache of pity for Roger who had striven to give people what they wanted. What an up-hill climb it must have been to have tried to be perfect for Albert's sake.

The door opened and Jane Brindle came in. "Albert," she began in her lovely voice.

He sat bolt upright in bed, a figure that should have been comic with the pipe-stem arms, the scrawny neck, the head too big for his body.

"No, Jane, no! I told Bessie not to let you come. I said I wouldn't see you."

She moved closer to the bed. "Albert," she said firmly, "you must not send me away. I can't —"

"Make her go," Albert appealed to Lois in frenzy. "Make her go!" He waved his hands, his lips moved but no more words came from them.

With a gesture of despair Jane went out of the room and Albert fell back on his pillows, his lips blue. Lois went quickly to the door.

"I think you'd better call a doctor," Lois said and Clyde picked up the telephone while Bessie went into the bedroom and closed the door.

She was still there when Dr. Thomas arrived. In the interval Jane had talked in a low tone to Clyde. The doctor looked around, his brows shooting up when he saw the first Mrs. Brindle.

"Well, Jane, good to see you. I heard you had come back. Planning to stay long?"

"Just a visit," she said.

He studied Clyde, a puzzled, speculative frown between his brows, and shot a sharp glance at Lois. Stirring things up, his expression said clearly. He was beaming when Bessie opened the bedroom door and came out.

"Well, Bessie, what's the trouble here? Tell Doc all about it."

Bessie's face was ravaged. "Albert is in a state of collapse. His heart is racing and he's an awful color. Like death. I can't understand it when he just lies there. What tires him so? And he keeps his door shut as though — as though we were to blame for — what happened."

"Anything special upset him?"

"Nothing reasonable," Bessie said. "He was talking to Mrs. Fleming when —"

The doctor turned to Lois and seemed about to speak. Then he picked up his bag, went into the bedroom and closed the door. After a few moments he opened it again.

"Need someone to give me a hand," he said and Clyde followed him into the bedroom. Almost immediately the boy came out.

"What was it?" his mother asked.

"I don't know. Dad — didn't want me around."

The color drained out of Bessie's face. Awkwardly she put her hand on his arm. "He's just sick, Clyde. Sick people are apt to get fancies."

He summoned up a smile that did not succeed in concealing his hurt. "Let's face it. Dad doesn't seem to like me very much."

Something broke in Bessie's face. "He does too like you," she said fiercely. "Anyone would like you. There's not a kinder, more considerate, sweeter-tempered boy —"

Clyde patted her head. "All right, Mom, skip it. If I can't do anything here —" he went out of the cottage, shoulders bent, a big, ungainly, slouching figure stamped with defeat.

"It's not fair," Bessie cried, "for Roger always to come ahead of Clyde. It's enough to make the boy bitter and —"

Jane dropped into a chair and lighted a cigarette. "You know, Bessie, there are times when I grow weary of having Roger blamed for everything that goes wrong. After all, Clyde owes him a great deal."

Bessie looked at her, opened her lips, did not speak. She smoothed down her apron with fingers that shook.

"And you've got a lot to answer for yourself, Bessie," Jane went on. "If Albert put Roger first, you've put Albert first. If any boy ever had to be satisfied with leftovers it's Clyde. And he is like his father in a lot of ways. You might think of that. Enormously like him."

Bessie's lips quivered and she pressed them hard together. For the first time Jane's face revealed neither compassion nor tolerance and Bessie seemed visibly to cower, shrinking from the woman who had been her lifelong friend.

Jane added abruptly, "Do you love the boy?"

Lois was paralyzed with embarrassment. This was the second time within an hour she had become involved in an intimate scene. She sat trying to look as though she were deaf and blind or, better still, as though she weren't there at all.

"Yes," Bessie said, choking. "Oh, yes! I guess I have kind of neglected him; I guess I have a lot of arrears of love to make up to him, but I do love him, Jane."

"Then, for God's sake, let him know it before it's too late," Jane said fiercely.

Dr. Thomas came out of the bedroom. "I've given Albert a hypodermic. He's asleep for awhile. But don't let anything get him excited again." He spoke to Bessie but his eyes were on Lois.

134

He shifted them to Jane. "And don't you make another attempt to see him, Jane. Doc's orders. I don't know what you are up to but ever since you reached Stoweville there's been gossip. You're trying your best to blacken the name of the finest man God ever made and I'm not going to let you do it."

Again Lois was conscious of the strong core of serenity in Jane's nature. Her strong hands were clasped loosely in her lap. Her big mouth had lost its lines of humor.

"I came to Stoweville," she said quietly, "to find the answer to a question. I won't be driven out until I find it."

"And what's the question?"

"Who turned on the gas heater in Roger's cottage the night he died."

"Roger," Doc said distinctly, "died of a heart attack in his own bedroom."

"Nothing of the sort," Jane said briskly, almost impersonally. "I know where he died and how. And I'm in this to the end. I'll fight if I have to."

There was no mistaking her intentions. Doc Thomas studied her, thinking hard. Then he flung out his arms in a gesture of surrender. "I don't know why you are doing this, Jane; why you couldn't let Roger rest in peace. But if you've got to know the truth, I'll tell you. I've tried my damnedest to protect his reputation. But if you want to smear him, I suppose you won't be satisfied until you succeed. Roger did it himself."

ELEVEN

The peace and quiet of the country, Lois thought savagely, as she walked along a path through the woods. I haven't encountered so many cross-currents of hatred since *Desire Under the Elms*.

The thought that plagued her, that drove her along the path, concerned her own responsibility in the matter. Had Roger Brindle taken his own life, as Dr. Thomas declared; or had he been murdered, as Shandy Stowe believed?

Lois came upon an irregular stone fence, looked cautiously around for snakes, and then perched on the fence while she lighted a cigarette. If it was murder she had the responsibility of any decent citizen. She couldn't sidestep it. People were becoming inoculated against their horror of the taking of human life. It had become mass production. But if you believed in anything at all, you had to believe that a killer must be stopped.

But why would anyone want to kill Roger Brindle, America's best-loved man; the man who, according to everyone, devoted his energies to trying to give people what they wanted. It was not for profit. No one gained financially; even his wife had been left almost without resources; and the people whom he had sheltered, as a stalwart tree shelters plants and vines, were left destitute. In a very real sense, everyone had lost by his death.

The crime itself was fiendishly clever because of its very simplicity. No clue. No weapon. A gas fireplace turned on. But why hadn't Roger noticed the odor of escaping gas? Even Doc Thomas could hardly have covered up a head injury if Roger had been knocked unconscious before the murder.

Lois shut her eyes to help her concentrate. Two nights before Roger's death an attempt had been made to shoot him. And no one had made any reference to the bullet hole through the window-pane. A fantastic conspiracy of silence. Two nights later someone had tried again. And succeeded. Not an impulsive crime, not the result of a moment of emotional storm. A patient business.

Carol? Carol who meant to marry Shandy and his money. Carol who had said clearly, "Hands off. This man is mine." But Ethel Hattery would not protect Carol. Never in the world. Unless she had been offered an extraordinarily high price for her silence. Would she protect her husband? Women were capable of queer, irrational loyalties, but loyalty to the execrable Joe at the expense of Roger —

Paula? Ridiculous. Self-centered, self-dramatizing, malicious, but not a killer. Anyone might shoot in a frenzy but the cautious turning on of the gas — no, not Paula.

The Kibbees? Not Albert, of course. Bessie, who did not attempt to conceal her hatred for

Roger, who blamed him for everything? No, she wouldn't hurt Albert that way. Unless she felt that only Roger's death would free Albert from his absorption in the man who was his hero.

Clyde? But no one, Lois realized, knows anything about Clyde.

Perhaps Dr. Thomas was right and Roger had killed himself. Certainly there was the internal evidence of his column, of his fatigue, of his loss of faith in his world; there was Jane's evidence of his depression, his secret drinking.

But someone had shot at him two nights before, shot at him with Shandy's missing gun. That was evidence that could not be argued away. Evidence of intention to kill.

The sun was hot on her back, the grateful warmth relaxed her tight nerves. The sky was a deep blue. The side of the hill had been cleared of trees and laid out in checkered fields, whose contrasting shades were like a pattern on the land, the fields separated from one another by low stone fences. In a hollow a dozen cows grazed. Big puffy white clouds floated idly. It was a pastoral scene at its best.

This was the place for meditating on Horace at his Sabine farm, not for speculations about murder. Lois shook her head impatiently, trying to free herself of emotions and to force her reluctant mind to grapple with its problems.

Reluctant? That was the chief difficulty, she acknowledged honestly to herself. She did not want to know about Roger's death. But she had to know. She could not evade her personal responsibility. It was clear that no one else intended to make any effort to uncover the truth. Don't stir things up, Dr. Thomas had warned her; Dr. Thomas who had risked his professional standing when he signed the death certificate, giving heart failure as the cause of death.

All right, Lois told herself angrily, stop hedging. Carol intends to marry Shandy, she made that clear this morning. And Shandy has stayed here all these years, in spite of the fact she jilted him, that she hurt him intolerably. And Joe Hattery is threatening Shandy. It was probably Shandy's gun that fired that shot at Roger. Or at least he believes it is.

She dropped her cigarette, put her foot on it and stood up, too restless to remain quiet any longer. But why did Ethel Hattery faint when Paula produced the gun? Ethel, who had, by all accounts, been Roger's mistress.

Lois began to walk again, almost running, as though trying to escape from her thoughts. Within a few moments she became aware that her heart was racing, that she was out of breath and trembling from exhaustion. After all, she had got up from a hospital bed only a short time before. Better take care or she would have a relapse and her slender reserve of money was exhausted.

She turned back, walking slowly. Why had Jane Brindle got her here? For the first time it occurred to her that Jane herself, as a successful magazine contributor as well as Roger's ex-wife, had undoubtedly been asked to write the series that had been turned over to her. Why had Jane passed the job on to someone else? Because Mignonne had talked of a ghostwriter who had a flair for people, for getting at the truth about them.

Lois started as a tiny toad made a long leap over her foot into the bushes. As she passed the Hattery cottage Joe came sauntering out to meet her. There was an ugly bruise on the side of his face and his jaw was swollen.

"What's going on at the Kibbees?" he asked. "Saw Doc come rushing out here a while ago."

"Mr. Kibbee had a sort of nervous collapse. He is better now."

"Plenty going on here," Joe said. He fell into step beside Lois. "Went by the big house a while ago and heard Mrs. Brindle and Paula having it out at the top of their voices. Could have heard 'em clear down in the village." He snickered. "Kind of late to be jealous, it seems to me. Brindle's no good to either of them now."

He gave Lois a side glance to see whether she appreciated the excruciating humor of this. She wanted to quicken her pace and get rid of him but her legs were trembling with weakness. Although there was no one in earshot, Joe spoke out of the side of his mouth, a habit, she assumed, that he had acquired in prison.

"Anyhow, Mrs. Brindle has got the wrong cat by the tail. Oh, maybe Brindle led the kid on; she's young and you can't blame a man for trying. But she wasn't the one."

"Joe!" Ethel Hattery was behind them, the pock-marks livid in her face, her mouth twisted, her eyes flaming. Why, Lois thought in a kind of shock, aware of the volcanic force of banked emotions, that woman is dangerous. Joe stood still, eyeing his wife warily. Obviously, he had not intended her to overhear his conversation with Lois. "Another word from you and I'll let you starve. I'll never give you another cent so long as you live. Is that clear?"

He shrugged, tried to laugh. All the essential weakness in his nature was apparent in his face and he was aware of it, humiliated, angry, impotent. He turned and flung off down the path.

The two women looked after him. Then the rage died out of Ethel's face. She looked spent. "Everyone talks," she said, her voice colorless. "Everyone made claims on Roger. But don't misunderstand. He wasn't in love with Paula; sorry for her, maybe, because she was left alone as he had been and she was crazy about him. He wasn't in love with Carol either; she was like a pretty kitten he stroked and gave a soft cushion by the fire. He wasn't — in love with me. Not really. Once I thought he was, but he was — just sorry."

Ethel was humble in her pain, a hopeless suffering too straightforward for embarrassment. "He was tired of all of us, tired in his very bones. In my opinion, he loved only one woman in his life and that was his first wife. And it's my guess she's the only human being who never made a

141

claim on him. We all — wanted too much."

She wheeled and went back to her cottage, a sloppy, white-faced woman, in whom even the anger had burned out.

In Roger's cottage Lois found a covered tray on the worktable. In spite of her anxiety over Albert, Bessie had not neglected to prepare lunch. When she had eaten it, Lois looked at her pile of notes and then stumbled out on the terrace, dragged the deckchair into the shade of the big elm and sprawled out.

Her eyes traveled up to the streaks of golden sunlight that played on the leaves, wandered down the sturdy trunk, fastened on the vine that coiled around it. Like Roger, she thought as she drifted toward sleep; the tree is like Roger and all these people were the vine that ended by strangling the tree.

ii

The tree was sturdy, but while she watched, a vine coiled around, strangling it. A woodpecker tapped at the rotten trunk, tapped and tapped. Then something closed over her shoulder.

"Mrs. Fleming! Mrs. Fleming!"

She awakened with a start. She was cramped and chilled through, bone cold. And it was dark. She had not expected the darkness. Of course, she had fallen asleep after lunch. She must have slept for hours. It was night now. The only light

142

was the circle at her feet where a flashlight shone down.

"Mrs. Fleming!"

She straightened up, her teeth chattering. "What is it?"

The flashlight tipped up, touching the homely face of Clyde Kibbee. "Are you all right?" He sounded worried.

"I must have fallen asleep. I'm half frozen, that's all." And a fool thing that was to do, she told herself. If I don't get another bout of pneumonia it will be undeserved luck.

He held out his hand and pulled her to her feet, so stiff that she could barely stand. "Come inside," he urged her. He plugged in the heater, opened the closet door and brought a coat which he wrapped around her.

"You are very thoughtful."

He looked concerned. "It's my fault. I should have looked out on the terrace for you before. I brought your dinner hours ago; when I couldn't find you I thought perhaps you were dining with Mr. Stowe. He's gone too."

Lois's teeth gradually stopped chattering, she huddled deeper in her coat, and then belatedly became aware of the inflection in his voice.

"Clyde! What's wrong? Why are you here at this time of night? What do you mean — he's gone too?"

"It's Paula," he told her. "Mrs. Brindle called our cottage a half hour ago to know whether Paula was with us. She's gone."

"Gone where?" Lois asked stupidly, still half drugged by her heavy sleep, still in a torpor as warmth began to creep over her.

"We don't know. She didn't take anything with her, no money, no clothes, nothing. She just ran away."

"What time is it?"

"Eleven-thirty."

"You're sure she didn't just go for a walk?" Lois realized how absurd the question was the moment she uttered it.

"She's terrified of the dark," Clyde said. "She keeps a night light burning because she's afraid to go to sleep in the dark. She must have been —"

"Been what?" Lois asked. The boy's white face worried her.

"Been more afraid of something else," he said bluntly. "If you're all right I'm going to look for her. Mrs. Brindle said I could take her car."

"Perhaps," Lois suggested, "Shandy is back. He's rather wonderful at finding people." She dialed 211 and rang three times. Almost at once Shandy's voice answered. She told him quickly what had happened.

"Clyde is taking Mrs. Brindle's car."

"I'll try the woods," Shandy said.

She spoke impulsively. "Let me go with you, Shandy. If she is afraid of someone, maybe it will help if I am there."

"Okay, I'll be down for you as soon as I throw on some clothes."

"Oh!" Lois said in surprise. "Had you gone to bed?"

"Long ago," he replied. "You get used to early hours in the country."

She put down the phone. "Shandy and I will try the woods. Don't wait, Clyde. I'm going to get on some warm slacks and a sweater. Two sweaters," she added, shivering again as the coat slipped off her shoulders.

"Paula would never go into the woods," Clyde said emphatically. "Never in this world. She's a timid little thing. She doesn't even step off the path in the daylight if she can help it."

"Has she any friends in Stoweville?"

"Mrs. Brindle is calling them."

Clyde went out and Lois heard him running toward the garage. Standing before the heater she put on black and white checked wool slacks, wool socks and sneakers, a white sweater and a red wool jacket. But all the time she dressed she wondered why Shandy had lied to her. She had not awakened him from a sound sleep. He had not gone to bed. A half-hour earlier, when Clyde had looked for him, he had not been home.

She saw a light moving along the ground and was waiting at the door when Shandy came up, a big lantern in his hand.

"Heavens, what a beacon!" she exclaimed. "You must have robbed a lighthouse."

"Never send a boy to do a man's work. What happened, do you know?"

"Only what I told you over the phone."

"Something must have set her off."

Lois thought of Paula brandishing the revolver which she claimed was Carol's and the expression on her face, half fear, half defiance. She thought of Joe smirking through his swollen face, while he told her of the quarrel he had overheard between Paula and Carol.

"Which way are you going?" she asked.

"Clyde will take the roads and he's so much in love with her that he won't miss a trick there. How long has she been gone?"

"Apparently no one has seen her since she went up to her room about nine-thirty."

"Two hours." Shandy stood with his head a little on one side while he considered. For the first time he resembled the Shandy of seven years before. Lois recognized the alert expression as he made his plans, considered the possibilities. How many times had they stood like this while Shandy weighed the evidence, studied his clues and decided on a course of action?

"We'll take the path back of your cottage," he said.

He walked ahead and Lois followed, her eyes on the broad path which his lantern made almost as bright as day. There were lights in the Hattery cottage and he knocked on the door.

Joe, in flamboyant pajamas, opened it. "You looking for her? Both Clyde and Mrs. Brindle called here but we haven't seen her." There was malice in his ineffectual face. "Nor heard her since she had that flaming row with Mrs. Brindle earlier

146

today." He stole a look at Shandy to see how he took this.

"Better get some clothes on," Shandy said shortly, "and search the woods to the left. Mrs. Fleming and I will bear right. Clyde's combing the roads."

"I wonder why Mrs. Brindle doesn't want to call the state police."

"We'll call the police if we don't find her in the next hour," Shandy said.

"We," Joe echoed.

It didn't seem possible that a one-syllable word could be packed with so much innuendo.

TWELVE

The woods were dark and the path was rough and worn. Even in wool clothing Lois was cold. Something threshed through the bushes and her heart was in her mouth. It's ridiculous to be afraid, she told herself. But the woods were inhabited by things she could not see. All around her there was invisible and hostile life. The fact that, by the sane light of morning, the lurking presence would resolve itself into nothing more menacing than gray squirrels was irrelevant. Her fear was so potent she could taste it.

Her foot caught on a vine and she stumbled. Ahead of her Shandy stopped. As he turned, the light fell on her face. "You look like the wrath of God," he told her bluntly. "I must have been crazy to let you come. I'm going to take you back to the cottage and go on alone."

"Nonsense, I'm perfectly all right," she retorted, ashamed. "Anyhow, we mustn't waste time. That child is out in the dark somewhere and she's afraid of it."

Shandy was callous to Paula's terrors. "She brought it on herself. Tearing off into the night like the heroine of a Gothic novel and expecting us all to go hunting for her. Do her good to get a first-rate scare."

"She's only seventeen," Lois pointed out.

"I don't know whether it's ever occurred to you that neurotic teen-agers provide the bulk of our young criminals." He added thoughtfully, "A girl like Paula has a lot of sentimentality fermenting in her but she is practically without moral scruples."

"Don't let Clyde hear you say that. He's infatuated with her."

"He could be infatuated with her and still know what she's like," Shandy commented. He laughed shortly. "You can admire a woman's virtues but you don't lose your head over them. At least," he added, "it isn't usual."

They had gone on some distance before he said, "At least, one gets over it. That's the saving grace. Like recuperating from a hangover."

He reached for her hand and his own was warm and reassuring. He noticed her labored breathing. "I'm an inconsiderate brute, dragging you along at top speed. Why didn't you tell me?" He walked more slowly now, sweeping the light from side to side, his hand holding hers, guiding her over the rough path.

"I agree with Clyde," Lois said suddenly. "Paula would never, never have come through these woods in the dark. And, anyhow, what made her run away? Who is she afraid of, Shandy? When she handed that gun to Mrs. Brindle —"

"What gun?" He was startled.

"I'd forgotten that you didn't know." Lois told him about Paula's explosive appearance, bran-

149

dishing the gun and thrusting it at Carol.

"What kind of gun, do you know?"

Lois tried to describe it.

"Where did Paula get it?"

"She didn't say."

"And she thought it was Carol's." Shandy said nothing more. He was absorbed, withdrawn, as though he were readjusting some theory he had already worked out.

"Shandy," she began.

"Shh!" He was standing still, listening. She heard it then, someone crying aloud. He moved the light to the right, to the left, held it there. Paula lay crumpled on the ground, crying loud and unrestrained like a baby. As the light touched her, she tried to burrow her head into the ground.

Lois ran forward. "Paula! It's Lois Fleming. You're all right. You're safe. Don't be afraid."

She knelt beside the girl whose tears caught in her throat. Paula lifted a face puffy from crying, the pale eyes red-rimmed, the lids inflamed. But she did not attempt to move.

"What is it?"

"I've broken my leg," she wailed.

They saw then the improbable angle at which her right leg was twisted. Shandy bent over her.

"I'll run back to the house and get a folding cot," he said quickly. "Joe can help me carry her back. That's about the best we can do." He felt in his pocket and pulled out a flask. "I thought we might need this."

He handed it to Lois who propped the girl's

head on her arm and made her take a couple of swallows of the brandy.

"You keep the lantern."

"But how will you manage?" Lois protested.

"I have a flashlight. I'll make it as soon as possible." As he started away, Lois called, "Ask Mrs. Brindle to call the doctor." He nodded, gave her a worried look and then went quickly, almost running, back along the path they had taken.

Lois crouched beside Paula. "We'll get you there just as soon as possible and the doctor will set your leg."

"And then I can't get away at all," Paula whimpered. There was mounting hysteria in her voice and Lois said sharply, "Stop that! I know it must hurt horribly but you won't help —"

"I don't want to go back to the house!" Paula clung feverishly to Lois's hand. "I don't want to."

"No one will hurt you," Lois said impatiently.

"You don't know. Carol hates me because of Roger. She tried to kill us both not two weeks ago. I'd gone to his cottage to see him and she shot at me through the window. I'm afraid."

"Carol. Oh, surely not." There was flat disbelief in Lois's voice.

Paula's forehead was beaded with perspiration from pain and Lois wiped her face gently and gave her another drink of brandy and still another. It would probably make her drunk but it was the only anaesthetic available and the child must be in agony.

"I know it was Carol. It had to be."

"Did you see her?"

"The window was dark. We couldn't see any-one. Only Roger thought it was Carol or he wouldn't have looked so queer; he wouldn't have made me promise not to say a word. He sealed over the hole. He looked so awful, so unhappy. It must have been Carol. And anyhow, no one else would care if Roger and I — and anyhow he was just — fatherly." Paula's voice broke and she began to cry again. "He — he — p — patted me on the head as if I was a baby," she wailed. "I told him how much I loved him and then someone shot right through the window at me. And it must have been Carol. And I wanted her to know I knew it. That's why I brought her the gun when I found it."

"Where did you find it?" Lois asked.

"On Roger's terrace. It was under the big elm tree, just covered over with earth."

Shandy's gun, Lois thought, feeling sick, and Shandy had a key to the gate in the fence. But it had not been Shandy on the terrace the night before, who had made his way so stealthily, so surely, through the dark room. No one could have taken the child's infatuation seriously unless — there was Ethel Hattery, of course, whom Roger had not merely patted on the head.

But it was Roger who had died. That bullet had been meant for Roger, not for Paula.

There were voices, footsteps, a gleam of light, and Shandy came in sight with Joe, carrying a folding cot. They opened it on the ground and lifted Paula. As they moved her she screamed once and fainted.

"Good," Shandy said in relief. "I hope she doesn't come around until we get her back to the house. We'll have to do some jolting on this path, no matter how careful we are, and it will hurt like hell." He took hold of his end of the cot. "All right, Joe. Easy does it. Try to hold it as steady as possible. Watch your footing. And if you drop your end, so help me God, I'll thrash you."

"You won't ever touch me again if you know what's good for you," Joe said harshly.

The trip back to the house took nearly half an hour. Paula was conscious, crying out with pain most of the time. The two men walked slowly, their eyes on the ground, so they would not stumble. Lois was at one side, holding the lantern. That was why she was the only one who saw the revealing shadows. The whole house was ablaze with light and the two shadows were thrown on the drawn white blind as clearly as though they had been projected on a movie screen: the thickset figure of Dr. Thomas, the slim silhouette of Carol Brindle, standing very close together. Then he pulled her violently into his arms, forced her head back, kissed her.

As the men's heavy tread sounded on the steps to the veranda the doctor's arms dropped to his sides. He was in the hall when the slow procession came in and followed it up the stairs to Paula's bedroom.

Carol, in a trailing green velvet negligee, was last to enter the room. When she offered to undress her niece the girl began to cry hysterically, "Don't touch me!"

Doc Thomas turned and gave Lois a steady look. Stirring things up, it said as clearly as though he had spoken the words aloud.

With some difficulty Lois got the girl's clothes off and slipped a nightgown over her head. Then she went to the door.

"All right," the doctor said cheerfully as he entered the bedroom, "Doc will look after you, young lady."

Carol was waiting with Shandy in the big library. She looked up when Lois came in.

"But what possessed her?" she asked helplessly. "What got into her?"

Shandy gave Lois a keen glance and shoved her unceremoniously into a chair. "You need a stiff drink." She shook her head. "Better not. I fell asleep after lunch and never woke up until Clyde came for me at eleven-thirty. I haven't had any dinner."

"I'll fix you something," he said. "You're ghastly. Just up from a sick bed yourself, and tearing around the country looking after other people. Won't take a minute."

Carol stirred in her chair. "I'll help," she offered.

"Stay where you are," Shandy said. "I know my way around this house."

Lois sank back in the chair into which Shandy

had pushed her and closed her eyes. She opened them at length with the uneasy feeling of being stared at. Carol did not look away at once.

"What a shame," she said graciously, "when you are employed to do some work that you should run into all our personal problems. I hope by tomorrow you'll be able to concentrate on your job."

The attack was petty; it was also unexpected. Lois realized that she had underestimated Carol who was prepared to take direct action to protect her property. Lois was aware that the yellow eyes did not miss the color that was rising in her face.

Shandy came into the room and thrust a glass into Lois's hand. "Scotch. Drink it. I'll have some food for you in a few moments."

"Please don't bother."

He winked at her and went out again. Lois sipped the scotch cautiously. In a few moments Dr. Thomas came down the stairs.

"She'll be all right," he told Carol. "I set the leg and gave her a hypodermic. She's drowsy and she'll be asleep before long. I'm leaving some pills in case she wakes up in pain. She can have one with water and another in four hours. It was a clean break and there's no reason for any complications."

He looked disapprovingly at the drink in Lois's hand, at her slacks, turned to Carol, fragrant and lovely and helpless in the extravagantly becoming velvet negligee. He likes the feminine type, Lois thought.

"All this has been too much for you. Would you like something to help you sleep?"

Carol shook her head, her eyes still on Lois. She stretched out in her chair. "I'm not going to bed yet. Anyhow, someone ought to stay with Paula in case she needs anything. And Bessie has her hands full with Albert."

"Paula's being — silly," the doctor said. "I'll get Ethel Hattery to stay with her tonight. Tomorrow, if you think it's a good idea, I'll try to get a nurse."

The outside door opened and Clyde came in. "I saw Doc's car. Did you find her? Is she all right? Is she hurt?"

"Paula is upstairs," Doc said. "She fell and broke her leg."

As Clyde started for the stairs Carol demanded, an edge of asperity in her voice, "Where on earth are you going?"

"I just want to look at her — to be sure —" Without waiting for a comment he ran up the stairs. They heard him open Paula's door, heard a harsh, wild scream. "Roger! Roger!"

Doc ran up the stairs, moving lightly for so heavy a man. "What did you do to her?" he snapped.

Clyde said slowly, "I don't know. I just looked in. I —"

"Get out of here!" Doc's voice changed as he spoke to his patient, became hearty again. "There now, nothing to take on about. Doc's here."

Clyde stumbled down the stairs. "Sit down,"

Lois said, in spite of the fact that Carol was waiting for him to leave. The boy was ghastly and at the breaking point. "Paula had just been given a hypodermic," she explained gently. "Probably her mind is confused, half dreaming. That's all there is to it. Now don't worry any more. She's safe and she's all right."

The boy looked at her dumbly, seeking reassurance, and found it in her eyes. "Thanks a lot," he said and went out.

Shandy brought in a tray with scrambled eggs, toast and coffee. Doc Thomas came down, gave Lois a hostile glance, looked lingeringly at Carol, curiously at Shandy, and took his departure.

Lois was ravenous. The drink, the hot coffee, the food restored her. She looked at her watch. "Good heavens, it's two-thirty!" She got up. "Shandy, you really saved my life."

"I'll take you home," he said.

Carol got lazily to her feet. "Darling, I'm sorry you should have responsibility for all these people practically thrust on you. But I don't know what I'd do without you. You always help me so much. After seeing Mrs. Fleming to her cottage, do get a good rest yourself."

He walked slowly beside Lois. "Feel better?" he asked.

"Quite all right."

"Did the kid tell you what was wrong?"

"She was with Roger Brindle the night someone shot through the window. She thought the bullet was meant for her. Evidently she has been brooding; she was afraid someone would try again and she got panicky." Why don't I say Carol, she wondered. Why am I so cautious?

Shandy opened the door of her cottage and followed her in. Recalling that from the second-floor windows of the big house the cottage could be seen, Lois said uneasily, "You had better go, Shandy."

Again his mind followed hers with uncomfortable fidelity. "Carol been making remarks?"

"Not exactly."

"That's all over," he told her abruptly. "I supposed you understood that."

Suddenly Lois was not tired at all. She felt young and light and quite irrationally happy but she managed to say levelly, "Does Carol understand it?"

Shandy made no direct answer. "Why did Paula scream tonight?"

Lois explained that Clyde had insisted on seeing her and that Paula in her drugged state had mistaken him for Roger or Roger's ghost and had screamed in terror.

Shandy shook his head. "I think you haven't quite got the picture. It is possible she was panicked by Clyde *in propria persona*. We might as well clear things as we go — you and I have a lot to clear up, Lois — so I'll tell you plainly I think it was Clyde Kibbee who fired that shot at Roger."

"Clyde! I simply don't believe it."

Clyde, Shandy explained, was an unknown factor. Because of Albert's frail health and his constant moving from church to church, he had never had a settled home; the boy had been kept away at schools and summer camps until he had gone into the army.

"He has been here only a few weeks," Shandy said, "and he fell for Paula right away. Paula, of course, had a kid's infatuation for Roger. I think the boy was blind jealous and a bit unbalanced by the war. Anyhow, his own father was so devoted to the great man he had no time for his own boy. Clyde has had a lot to resent."

"You mean he killed Roger?" Lois was incredulous.

"Oh, no," Shandy said. "I don't think there was any connection —" His voice trailed off and he looked down at her. "We'll talk about it tomorrow." He started for the door, wheeled, returned to her, gathered her into his arms and kissed her, eyes, cheeks, throat, lips, until she was limp, clinging to him. No moment will ever again be like this, she thought.

He released her with such abruptness that she staggered. "And I thought you'd come too late!" He went out, closing the door behind him.

THIRTEEN

The sheet of paper was adorned only by a half-dozen lines which had been x'd out. As blank as my mind, Lois thought. She was uncomfortably warm again and for the third time got up to switch off the electric heater. She returned to stare at the accusing page of paper in her typewriter and then, as a shiver ran along her spine, turned the heater on once more.

What kept her sitting in front of the silent typewriter was her respect for deadlines. In six weeks she must have finished copy on the first article in the hands of the editor, with the others following at weekly intervals. By now she should have been able to produce a detailed outline. Half a dozen glib openings had already suggested themselves but she felt a curious sense of obligation to Roger Brindle. He deserved better at her hands. He had spent his life giving people what they wanted and someone had killed him. Someone had entered this very room and turned on the gas.

The gate in the fence creaked and she turned swiftly to see Shandy coming across the terrace. He waved to her and came on, smiling. When he opened the Dutch door and came in the smile faded. For a moment he studied her, dark head a little on one side, hands in the pockets of his slacks. He wore a sport shirt with an open collar and looked younger than she had ever seen him, younger even than he had been seven years earlier. There was a new air of determination about him and instinctively Lois found herself gathering her defenses.

"It's all right to be a ghost but isn't it carrying matters a bit far to look like one?" he inquired. "You are too pale and there are shadows under your eyes." With his fingertips he touched one cheek. "You're cold!"

He picked her up unexpectedly, put her on the couch and drew over her a Scotch plaid blanket. "Too much romping around in the woods for you last night. Take it easy for the rest of the day."

"But I have work to do," she answered him helplessly.

"And time to do it in."

"After all, you know, I'm not here as a guest," she reminded him.

He shot her a quick, speculative glance, opened his lips and closed them again. He looked at the paper in her typewriter. "At least," he commented, "you can't pretend that I interrupted any flow of ideas." He sat down at the typewriter and began to poke at the keys in two-fingered, plodding fashion, his forehead puckering as he concentrated on his work.

"What on earth are you doing, Shandy?"

"Borrowing your typewriter. I want to get off

161

that advertisement for Ethel Hattery. Should have done it before but what with one thing and another —" he swiveled around in the chair and grinned at her. "You are a very distracting person to have around, Lois. Bad for my peace of mind."

To her intense annoyance Lois could feel herself blushing. "Speaking of the Hatterys," she began quickly.

His dark brows arched. "Were we?" he asked in amusement.

"Shandy — did you fight with Joe Hattery?"

His grin faded. "I just explained, in the only way that septic little rat would understand, that I don't like Peeping Toms."

Remembering how she had stood unclothed in the brightly lighted room with the dark windows, dropping the filmy nightgown over her head, she shrank back, her face dark with color. "Is that what — ?"

"That's what he was doing outside your cottage the night you came. I'm sorry it happened, Lois, but I can guarantee it won't happen again."

"You've made an enemy on my account," she said uneasily, remembering Joe's voice the night before.

"The world is Joe's enemy," he told her dryly. "And someone should have dealt with him a long time ago." His dark eyes were troubled. "Look here, Lois, you'd better let Doc take a look at you."

"Not Dr. Thomas," Lois said firmly. "He probably sits on his patient to saw off a leg. Anyhow, he regards me as Public Enemy Number One."

"Well, of course," Shandy said, "he has a point there."

"He told Jane Brindle that Roger had killed himself."

After a startled look, Shandy turned his back to her and began poking at the keys. It was a stiff, almost a hostile back.

"First it was a heart attack," Lois said. "But he knew he couldn't fool Jane about that. So now it is suicide. Who is the man protecting, Shandy, at the expense of his friend's reputation?"

He pushed back the big chair that had been Roger's and stood beside the couch, looking down at her. She found herself wishing that she could see behind the shining surface of his eyes.

"Let this alone, Lois. Let it alone."

"I can't," she said helplessly. "There has been a crime and no one is doing anything about it. You are all covering up."

His eyes were very bright. "Let it alone," he said again. "Perhaps then we'd have a chance."

"Who would?"

"You and I." He went back to the typewriter, poked at the keys. At length he yanked the paper out of the machine. "How's this?" he asked in his usual voice and read aloud:

WANTED: an employer to whom Ethel Hattery can give the same faithful service as a secretary that she gave to Roger Brindle.

163

"That ought to bring results," Lois said. In answer to a tap on the door she called, "Come in."

This morning Ethel Hattery's skin looked gray with fatigue. Her mouth, without make-up, was blue white. There were hollows under her eyes.

"Anything I can do for you?" she asked. "Any typing?"

"You are exhausted," Lois exclaimed. "Have you had any rest?"

"I'll rest now if you don't need me. Dr. Thomas just left. Paula's pretty uncomfortable, of course, but she had a fair night and she'll be all right. Mrs. Kibbee is going to keep an eye on her this morning."

"Did you sit up all night?"

Ethel nodded. "I didn't mind. I haven't been sleeping much anyhow the last few weeks."

Shandy handed her the advertisement he had written. "I'll try this on the metropolitan papers, Ethel. You ought to get something pretty good out of it, enough offers so that you can pick and choose."

The secretary read it through twice. "That's rather clever of you," she remarked at length tonelessly. She handed back the sheet of paper and her eyes traveled around the cottage as though saying good-by with a kind of dumb pain. "But will anyone else put up with Joe?"

"Get rid of him," Shandy advised her.

Ethel's expression was sardonic. "You needn't be afraid."

Shandy ignored her mocking tone. "I meant it. He's no good to himself and no good to you. There's no earthly reason for carrying that burden around with you."

"You know I can't get rid of him now. I'll never be able to leave him now." Her feet dragged as she went to the door. "How glad you'll all be to be free of us." For a moment she stood on the threshold, her back to them. "Particularly you," she said.

When she had gone, Lois sat up, throwing off the blanket.

"Stay where you are," Shandy insisted. He was beside her in an instant, his hand on her shoulder, pressing her down.

She shook it off. "I'm tired of being muzzled."

He grinned at her. "Though you can fret me —"

"I don't want to pluck out the heart of your mystery," she flamed.

The smile deepened. "Don't you?"

The room seemed too close, too small. Instinctively, Lois put up her hand as though to ward him off. "Shandy, why did Joe Hattery go to prison?"

"Extortion."

"So that's it!"

"All right," he said grimly. "There are some things you had better understand. I know, as well as I know that you are here in this room, making your hair stand on end by running your fingers through it, that Roger Brindle was murdered. The night he died I dropped in to see him about

165

eleven-thirty. I recognized my own symptoms enough to know I was going to have a sleepless night and his lights were still burning. Roger was one of the people I didn't mind having see me. I came down, as I often did, to talk to him. He was lying on the couch with his head flung back so that it was clear off the pillow, out like a light, dead drunk. When he was found the next morning he was lying in exactly the same position. He had never moved. I could swear to that. But, meantime, the gas fireplace had been turned on and not lighted. Roger could not have turned it on and put himself back in exactly the same position."

Shandy paced up and down the room. "You are wondering why I didn't say anything. Well, the first thing I heard, after being told of Roger's death, was that he had died of a heart attack. That was Doc Thomas's doing. And the day of Roger's funeral Joe Hattery dropped in to see me. Joe had quite a case against me. He had seen me go into Roger's cottage the night he died; he knew that someone had shot at Roger two nights before and I'm the only person on the place who has a gun; he knew I had been engaged to marry Carol before she — decided on Roger."

"He wanted money?"

"He wanted money," Shandy said.

"You wouldn't be such a fool —" Lois began in alarm.

"No," Shandy assured her, "I wouldn't."

166

"Are you positive that it was your gun?"

He shrugged. "The bullet was a .22. My gun was a .22. I'm reasonably sure that's the one Paula unearthed. I'd give a lot to be able to question her." He offered Lois a cigarette, lighted it and one for himself and strolled over to the Dutch door. He said lightly, "The tiresome part of the business is that the gun seems to have disappeared again."

Lois's hands were rigid. "But, Shandy," she half whispered. "But, Shandy."

"Is there any reason," he demanded, "why you have to work here? Can't you take the material back to New York and write in your own apartment? Do you have to stay?"

"Aren't you being rather melodramatic?"

"I don't like disappearing guns," he said stubbornly.

"But, I — but nobody — oh, Shandy, this is really nonsense. I'm no danger to anyone."

"You were never," he told her oddly, "more mistaken in your life." He drew her to her feet. "Lois," he said and pulled her into his arms and kissed her. "Lois, I'm terribly in love with you. I don't want to talk about Roger any more. I want to talk about you and me." He released her abruptly. "I didn't realize how done up you are. Trust Stowe to pick the wrong time. Come on."

Ignoring her protests, he settled her in the long chair on the terrace and brought out the Scotch plaid blanket which he wrapped around her. "Stay

167

here and rest," he ordered. "Don't worry. Don't think about anything. Anything at all. I'll retype the advertisement and send it off." He bent over and his lips brushed her forehead. Then he went inside.

Lois lay with closed eyes, listening to the leaves stirring with the breeze, feeling the sun warm on her face. Sick at heart. How could I have been such a fool, she thought; believing he was in love with me. Responding like a naive girl. And he's trying to sidetrack me. But what an unforgivable way to silence me. How could he.

She drifted into an uneasy sleep. Somewhere a door opened and closed. High heels clicked over the floor. Carol's voice said, "You here, darling? Where's Mrs. Fleming?"

"Asleep on the terrace. I'm typing Ethel's advertisement."

"How kind you are! I couldn't get along without you, Shandy."

Something in the magnolia soft voice made Lois open her eyes. I must let them know I am awake, she thought. I'm not supposed to hear this.

Shandy hit a few more keys on the typewriter and pulled out the page. "That's the lot. I thought I'd put them in all the New York papers."

"Thank you. I've said that to you so long, so often. Just thank you. But at last you know I'll be able to thank you better now, differently — after all these years you've waited."

"Steady, Carol," Shandy said quickly, warningly.

"Anyhow," she ignored the interruption, "anyhow, darling, something rather — frightening has happened. We'd better not say anything, just at present."

"Say anything about what?"

Carol's voice hardened imperceptibly. "About the fact that we are going to marry."

Lois stumbled to her feet. I've got to stop them, she thought, appalled.

It was already too late. Shandy was standing at the Dutch door and his face was horror-struck when he saw that she was awake.

FOURTEEN

Lois turned without a word and crossed the terrace. Shandy had left the gate unlocked when he came in. She went through and closed it behind her. She walked blindly, eager only to put as much distance as possible between her and the man and woman in Roger's cottage. Poor Roger, she thought in a kind of outrage, and was surprised at her own partisanship for the man who would not stay dead. Poor Roger.

It was her stricken pity for him that led her to Albert Kibbee's cottage. There, at least, she would find a loyalty that had never wavered; a loyalty touched with hysteria, perhaps, but one on which Roger could have relied.

The door was open and Bessie sat crumpled in a chair, her eyes empty as she stared at the wall. Over night the precarious balance between middle age and old age had been altered. Bessie's face sagged, the very texture of her skin seemed to have changed. The sturdy body had collapsed on itself.

Lois paused. She could not intrude on that mute despair. What poet had said, 'Hopeless grief is passionless'? The tragedy in Bessie was too deep, too irremediable for pain. But part of her had died.

Before Lois could turn away, Bessie looked up. Her voice, like her eyes, was dulled, but habit asserted itself. "Come in, Mrs. Fleming." She got to her feet and bustled around, straightening an ornament that had already been arranged with military precision.

"Am I disturbing you?"

Bessie shook her head. "I was just sitting here," she said, as though surprised by her own inactivity. "Let me make you some tea. You could take a cup to Albert." She lifted her apron to wipe away an imaginary spot of dust from a bowl on the table. "He won't let me in. Maybe he'd take it from you." She stood looking aimlessly at Lois, a woman ill at ease when she was not busy but with her occupation momentarily stripped from her.

"Clyde's gone off," she said. "He's been away all morning. He can't get over frightening Paula. I could shake that girl though I realize she was too sick to know what she was doing. But Clyde can't seem to understand that's all there was to it. He thinks no one likes him, not even Albert." She added flatly, "It's not good for him. You're lucky not to have anyone, Mrs. Fleming, I can tell you. It's terrible to love people and not be able to help them. It's just plain awful."

When the tea had been prepared, accompanied by fragrant cinnamon toast, Lois took the tray Bessie had fixed with anxious care and tapped at Albert's door.

"Who is it?" inquired the reedy voice.

"Lois Fleming." When he had unlocked the door she set the tea tray on a table beside his bed, filled a cup for him and stood hesitating.

He ignored the tea. "Sit down," he said. There was none of the eagerness she had seen in him on her arrival. "Mrs. Fleming," he demanded, ignoring the tea, "why are you doing this?"

"Doing what?" she asked in honest surprise.

"Stirring things up. Doc was here yesterday when I had the attack. He told me that you are a troublemaker, trying to hurt Roger's reputation."

Lois was so angry for a moment that she could not speak. Then she said quietly, "I haven't the slightest intention of stirring things up, as Dr. Thomas says. But even if I did, it would be better than covering them up. There is no possible justification for the way he has behaved, either as a physician or as a friend. He ought to lose his license for it. He knew as well as the rest of you, better than most of you, that Roger Brindle did not kill himself. For him to say so is a contemptible lie. That's what I call stirring things up, Mr. Kibbee. Leaving a scar on Roger Brindle's reputation. I came here to try to get a picture of the man and to give that picture to the people all over the country who loved him. All I have met with is evasions. Dr. Thomas is deliberately covering up the fact that his friend was murdered and at the same time attempting to make me believe that Mr. Brindle was responsible for his own death."

Albert sat bolt upright in bed. "But I thought," he said, shocked and bewildered, "Roger's heart failed. I don't understand any of this."

There was no indication that he was in danger from another collapse. He was alert, intent, ready for action. Perhaps, Lois thought, he would be better off if his wife would let him get up than if she continued to keep him penned in bed, where he could do nothing but brood. True, he had no strength but he had the wiry kind of energy that often outlives the sturdy, athletic kind.

"I thought you knew," she said in apology. "I thought all of you knew. I am sure Mrs. Brindle does because she was so afraid to have me use the gas fireplace."

"Was that — what did it?"

She nodded.

Albert Kibbee was silent for a long time but it was the silence of an active mind, thinking intently. "Someone killed Roger," he said at last, speaking tentatively, as though testing the words, the idea. "Killed him." After a pause he said, "Wanted him dead," and listened to the words.

"That's not possible, Mrs. Fleming." He sounded reassured, convinced of the preposterous nature of the idea. "Simply not possible."

He looked at her with his clear, direct gaze, saw her expression and his eyes clouded. "Don't you see," he said persuasively, "no one disliked Roger. He was — he was — if you could only have known him."

"But someone disliked him very much," Lois insisted. "And I can't just stand back. You must see that."

"Yes," he said gently. "I see that. Gas, you say. And Carol knows?" He was silent for a long time. "Not Carol," he said at length. "Not Carol, Mrs. Fleming. She doesn't have very deep emotions and as long as she was sure of her comforts — and she would always have been sure with Roger — she would never have done that. Never. Anyhow, she appreciated him. She helped him to realize what he was. Not like Jane. Or Paula Case. Paula is very different from her aunt. She's no good. She pursued Roger in the most shameless —" his voice shook. "There's evil in her. See the way Clyde follows her like a dog. Why can't he let her alone?"

"They are both young," Lois pointed out. "And your son is a lonely boy. Such a terribly lonely boy."

Albert's eyes were as blue as a midsummer sky. "Like father — like son. I am afraid I have been unforgivably slow in seeing Clyde as he really is." He was looking at some inner vision of his own. "Mrs. Fleming," he said urgently, "it's important that Clyde should not grow bitter and resentful. I hardly know — what he is capable of." His voice rose higher. "Find him for me, Mrs. Fleming. I want to see him."

Bessie, busily darning stockings, looked up quickly as Lois came out of the bedroom.

"He wants me to find Clyde," Lois told her

174

in a low tone. "He wants to see him at once."

An expression of almost incredulous hope dawned on Bessie's face. Then it faded. "Clyde's such a good boy," she said. "So — gentle." Automatically she dropped the darning egg into the heel of a sock, her hands shaking. "He went into the woods, up where you found Paula. Just because she went there the place is important, all of a sudden."

Impulsively Lois put a hand on the plump shoulder. "Don't worry. I'll find him and send him home."

"I don't know if I want you to," Bessie said and bent over her darning, her chin quivering.

ii

As Lois climbed laboriously up the path through the woods, Clyde came to meet her. It occurred to her that she had not worked out a plan of campaign. She was unprepared, and yet something must be done at once. Because Shandy's gun was missing.

She sat down on a fallen log and at her gesture of invitation Clyde sat on the ground beside her, clasping his knees in his big bony hands. Nature was really unfair, Lois thought, endowing Roger with so much charm and Clyde with none at all, when otherwise they were not unlike physically.

"I came to find you," she said at length. "Your father wants to see you. I think it has occurred to him rather belatedly that he hardly knows you."

"Now that Roger is gone," Clyde said grimly.

"Don't hate him so!" Lois did not know that she was going to say the words until they had been spoken.

Clyde looked up at her, a mirthless smile touching his big mouth. "Even dead I mustn't hate him. And he took everything I had: my father, my mother, my home, my girl — though I never had her really." He shifted his position so that his face was hidden. "Summers and vacations when other kids could go home I'd stay at school. I couldn't go home because it was Roger Brindle's home and there was no place for little boys. He might be disturbed. I used to lie awake nights planning what I would do to him when I was big enough. Do you know how many ways there are of killing? It's really a fascinating subject. I thought of dozens. I pictured doing each one of them — in detail. Of course, after I got into the army I discovered a lot I'd never thought of." He could keep his voice light but he could not keep it steady.

Listening to the thin voice of hate, Lois was appalled. What had Roger Brindle done to this boy? How much of this was words, how much a corrosion of the spirit? It is hard to sympathize with anything as ugly as hate. She wanted to sympathize, to understand, to reach the boy's bitter loneliness, but she remembered the man who had breathed gas while he lay asleep.

"And now I've come back mother is ashamed

of me. She keeps me out of sight. And Dad hates me because I am alive and Brindle is dead."

"Clyde," Lois said abruptly, "do you know how Roger Brindle died?"

"Thinking noble thoughts," Clyde said with a sneer.

"He was drunk when he died," she told him. "Drunk because it was the only way he could escape from his constant failure to achieve the perfection other people forced on him. So drunk that he could not have turned on that gas fireplace. He died because someone wanted him to die."

He did not move. She heard one sharply drawn breath. Nothing more.

"Drunk," he said at last in a tone of disbelief. The fact of Roger being drunk seemed more incredible than the fact of his being murdered. He began to laugh. "Galahad high! Santa Claus tipsy! Bayard's face on the barroom floor. O God, how marvelous!" He rocked with his wild laughter. "Does Paula know her plumed knight had a load on?"

Lois gripped his shoulder. "Clyde," she snapped, "stop acting like a jealous fool and listen to me. I said that he was murdered! Do you understand?"

The eyes that were too small for his big face, the eyes that were so like Bessie's, met hers without wavering. "Murdered," he repeated. As he said it, it was a word like any other. "So what?" The attempt at flippancy failed miserably.

"We can't let it go," Lois said distinctly. "Not murder."

"But Dr. Thomas couldn't possibly have made a mistake like that."

"He didn't make a mistake. He knows Roger was killed."

"But Doc wouldn't take a chance on covering up for anyone," Clyde protested. He added slowly, "Except Mrs. Brindle, perhaps. Or himself, of course."

"I wonder if you know that Paula ran away because she was afraid. Someone shot through the window two nights before Roger died, when Paula went to see him in his cottage. There was no harm done, you've got to believe that; a young girl's infatuation for an older man who never encouraged her, who refused to take her seriously. She told me that herself. It's true. But someone wanted him to die for that."

Clyde's face tightened, His eyes were on his clasped hands. He did not raise them.

"Clyde," Lois said urgently, "we can't let it go, you know. Because the gun has disappeared."

Still he did not move but, behind his closed face, his thoughts were racing. And quite suddenly he was afraid. She knew when the fear hit him.

He swung up to his feet, towering over her. "Mrs. Fleming, if you are worried about Paula, I promise you that nothing will happen to her. She's all right. But drop this now." His voice was so quiet that there was an interval before she realized that it was also threatening.

She turned and went back down the path, aware that he was watching her. She controlled an impulse to run.

iii

And there was no place for her to go. She had to get out of the woods and away from Clyde Kibbee. She could not return to her cottage because of the man and woman whom she had left there. Where then? Jane, she thought. It's time Jane Brindle and I have this thing out.

When she reached the village inn there was no one in the big lobby, one section of which was set with small cocktail tables, the other with easy chairs grouped around an outsize fireplace. She touched a bell on the small table which held the registration book and, while she waited for someone to come, shut herself in the telephone booth to call Mignonne. As she started to drop a coin in the box she recalled that this was the literary agent's day out of her office and for a moment she was bitter with frustration.

Someone was moving across the big lobby and she looked out, expecting to see the manager of the inn. Joe Hattery came in sight, around the corner that led to the staircase and the bedrooms of the guests on the second floor.

There was no reason, of course, why he should not be in the inn. What held her attention was the way he looked carefully around the room and then let himself out a side door onto the wide lawn running down to the river that was one of the features of the inn. Lois came out of the telephone booth and reached a window in time to see him dart out of sight around the side of the building.

She turned to meet the smiling inquiry of the manager, a pleasant woman in her forties.

"Mrs. Jane Brindle? Oh, yes. She is our only guest at the moment. She has the corner room at the end of the corridor, Number Fourteen. You can't miss it."

Lois went up the stairs and found Number Fourteen. Jane was there. Lois could hear her pacing up and down the room. She tapped and the sound within stopped abruptly. Lois had a curious conviction that the woman inside waited as she was waiting. She tapped again and called, "Mrs. Brindle?"

At the sound of her voice the door opened promptly and Jane Brindle smiled at her. "Come in, Mrs. Fleming. How nice of you." But the hand she held out was unexpectedly cold. She indicated a chair and then, with a murmured apology, lifted off the clothes that were piled on it. Lois observed that a suitcase was open on the luggage rack.

"Am I interrupting you?"

Jane seemed to bring her mind back from a long distance. "No," she said vaguely. She pushed a pile of underwear to one side and sat on the edge of the bed. "There's no hurry about this."

"Are you leaving Stoweville?"

"Yes," Jane said. "I'm going back to New York." She offered Lois a cigarette and lit one for herself. She was not, Lois realized, going to be helpful.

"Mrs. Brindle," she asked, "why did you want me to come here? What did you expect of me?"

Jane considered her question thoughtfully. She was an odd color. She's in a state of shock, Lois thought. Something has happened to her. She wondered how much it had to do with Joe Hattery making his furtive exit from the inn, Joe who had said, "The first Mrs. Brindle's done very well, hasn't she?" Joe, who had served a prison term for extortion.

"You are very forthright, aren't you?" Jane said at length with a faint smile.

"It's about time someone was," Lois retorted. "And the whole thing was pretty obvious when I began to think about it. I mean, that you must have been the one the magazine wanted for those articles, that you persuaded Mignonne to put me on the job instead. Why did you want me to come here, Mrs. Brindle?"

Jane made no reply. She seemed to have withdrawn into her own thoughts.

"You answered that, of course," Lois persisted, "when you told Dr. Thomas you wanted to know who turned on that gas fireplace. But — just what did you expect me to do?"

"I don't know," Jane said at last. "Honestly,

181

Mrs. Fleming, I don't know." She added, "I think I was afraid. Because Roger wouldn't have killed himself. And murder —" She got up from the bed and began to walk aimlessly from window to window. It was the first time Lois had seen her stripped of her serenity, of the quality of repose that seemed an essential part of her nature. She turned suddenly. "Please believe me, it wasn't —" she groped for a word — "it wasn't revenge, an eye for an eye, anything like that." After a long time she repeated, "I was afraid."

"What did you expect of me?" Lois asked again.

"You can get at people," Jane said after a troubled silence. "I wanted — I needed — to know —" her voice trailed off.

"What?"

"Whether Roger's death was the end or the beginning. I — have to know. Murder doesn't — just stop. And from the beginning I was sure it was murder."

Lois caught sight of herself in the mirror, slim in tailored slacks, her dark curly hair ruffled from the fingers she had been running through it, eyes too big for the thin face and much too bright.

"Dr. Thomas lied, of course," she said. "Roger was drunk that night." She repeated Shandy Stowe's story. "And Joe Hattery is trying to blackmail Shandy."

Jane's eyes flickered but she made no comment.

Lois tried then to give an orderly report. She told Jane about the shot that had been fired through the window in Roger's cottage, about

Ethel smashing the windowpane and Shandy taking the bullet, about Paula finding the gun and its subsequent disappearance. She told her about Paula's attempt to run away from Carol and her scream of horror when Clyde went up to see her, about Ethel Hattery fainting when the gun appeared, about Albert hearing the truth in regard to Roger's death and his demand to see Clyde.

When she finished, Lois waited for Jane to comment. Instead, Jane asked her, "What do you think of Clyde Kibbee?"

"Suppose," Lois said, "you answer a question, Mrs. Brindle." She could feel the older woman gather her defenses. "How did you know about the gas fireplace?"

"I got a letter," Jane told her reluctantly. "An anonymous letter."

"Did you keep it?"

Unexpectedly Jane smiled. "Oh, it wasn't necessary. I knew who it was from. She forgot I'd remember her handwriting. She was always a stupid woman. Anyhow, jealousy makes a woman do stupid things."

"What should we do now?"

"I know what I'm going to do," Jane said grimly. "I'm staying here. And I'm going to see Clyde Kibbee."

Not until she was walking back to the house did Lois realize that Jane had told her nothing at all.

FIFTEEN

That afternoon Carol sent for Lois. Her voice over the telephone was pleasant but it was the voice of an employer.

"I thought," she said, when Lois joined her in the library, "you'd want to get some work done for a change. That is, you must find it awfully disagreeable to get so involved in our affairs. I know how I should feel if I were to get all mixed up in something that was not my concern."

For several hours she talked while Lois made notes. There was no reference to the scene in the cottage, to the conversation which Lois had inadvertently overheard, but it stood between the two women like a wall. When Carol had stopped talking there was a brief interval of silence. Then she said, still in that soft voice of hers, "I thought I'd give you all the information I have so you can take the material back to New York with you to work it up."

"Any way you like," Lois replied, trying to keep her voice casual. She longed to be able to say, "I won't go on with this," but she thought of Roger sleeping away his life in the cottage and set her teeth.

Carol leaned back lazily, smiling at her. "That would probably be best," she said. "And would you mind if Bessie gives you dinner on a tray after this? Since my great sorrow I find it trying to talk to strangers." She nodded her dismissal and Lois went back to the cottage, raging.

Clyde brought her tray that evening, set it down without a word and went out. Pariah, Lois thought ruefully. She finished typing her notes and tried to read but her attention was not on the printed page. When she became aware that she was waiting for Shandy, expecting him to come, to explain that scene of the morning, she slammed the book shut and turned on the radio so she could no longer listen for the creak of the gate and the sound of his halting footsteps.

As the evening grew chilly she plugged in the electric heater. And she must have dozed. Because it was that night the attempt was made, which so nearly succeeded, to kill her.

For Lois there was a nightmare, sharp and horrible and terrifying, in which Clyde Kibbee chased her through the woods. She was unable to run because her feet were entangled in creeping vines and undergrowth. And Paula was screaming in terror, "Roger! Roger!" Then there was nausea, there were lights and voices and people doing disagreeable things to her helpless body.

When she became conscious she looked up through a slit between her eyelids. She was lying on the couch. Dr. Thomas, his face wet with sweat, his sleeves rolled up, was bending over her. And the cottage seemed to be filled with women. Carol was there and Bessie Kibbee and

185

Ethel Hattery. Lois was wrapped in blankets because the windows and doors were wide open. Even so the air was permeated with the odor of gas. And even yet she did not understand. It was only when Ethel automatically picked up a cigarette and reached for a match that she knew.

"Don't light that!" the doctor shouted at her. "The room is still filled with gas."

She knew then that someone wanted her to die. She closed her eyes on that knowledge while she tried to understand it. But why, she thought. Why? If I knew who had killed Roger, there would be some reason; but I don't know.

Someone wants me dead, she told herself. And the words were meaningless. Someone here. Perhaps someone in the room with me at this moment.

She opened her eyes the merest slit and looked through her lashes from face to face. Ethel's pock-marked face was white and drawn with fatigue. She had been nursing Paula, Lois remembered. Bessie's small eyes were sunken in her head. New lines had come into her face. She seemed half dazed. Carol, shivering in a pale blue satin house coat, was helpless as usual. Of them all, Dr. Thomas looked the worst. Lois had the curious impression that he was deliberately restraining himself from looking at Carol but that his attention was riveted on her.

Lois closed her eyes tightly. Which one, she thought. Which one?

"But I told her not to use the fireplace," Carol

said. She sounded exasperated. "I sent her the electric heater. I told her the fireplace was — dangerous."

In her anger Lois felt her heart begin to pound. Dr. Thomas, his fingers on her pulse, felt it too.

"She's conscious," he said. And as Lois was forced to open her eyes he bent over her. "Mrs. Fleming," he said slowly, distinctly, "why did you do it?"

It was a moment before Lois grasped the incredible words, before she understood fully what he was attempting to do. Then she tried to sit up and was violently sick.

When the paroxysm was over she lay back exhausted. "I didn't turn on the heater," she said then. "Someone tried to murder me the same way Roger Brindle was murdered."

The words had been spoken at last. And quite suddenly Lois was afraid. For there was something in the room that threatened her.

It was Carol who said, "She's out of her mind."

Lois forced herself to sit up, in spite of her weakness, in spite of the waves of blackness that kept moving through her head and blotting out her vision.

"I am perfectly sane," she said, aware that her voice was thick, the words indistinct. "If there's any question about that, I want another doctor. And I want a policeman."

Dr. Thomas shifted his stand with lightning speed. Incredibly, he was beaming at her. "You lie down, young woman," he said in his hearty

187

bedside manner. "Doc's orders. Ethel will get you undressed."

Ethel looked at Lois thoughtfully. "I've got to get back to Paula," she said and left the cottage before Dr. Thomas could make a protest.

"Bessie?" he asked. There was no question of expecting any exertion from Carol Brindle.

"I'll do it," Bessie said flatly.

"In the morning," the doctor told Lois, "after a good night's sleep you'll be more — we'll see about all this." He took Carol's arm gently and led her away.

Bessie knelt down and took off Lois's shoes. "I'll get you ready for bed." Shock had emptied her voice and her eyes of expression. She put the shoes neatly in the closet. "Did you see — anything?"

"No one," Lois said almost too quickly because she was, unreasonably, afraid of Bessie.

"Not being well, I guess you got confused like," Bessie said.

They can't do this, Lois thought. I've got to call the police and another doctor, a doctor who isn't hypnotized by Carol, a doctor who isn't trying to cover up. But she remembered her own blurred voice. She would not make a good or a convincing impression if she wanted to assure anyone tonight of her clear intelligence. Better wait.

Bessie pulled off her socks and her slacks.

"What happened?" Lois asked, her voice still thick, the words still blurred.

Bessie did not look up. "Ethel found you. She heard the radio, saw the lights and came in. She called the rest of us. Fortunately, Shandy knew what to do or you'd have been dead before Doc got here. Said he had a flat tire. Anyhow, he took his time."

She hung up Lois's clothes, brought her a nightgown and opened the bed while Lois sat in a chair.

"Why?" Lois asked at length.

Bessie bent over, smoothing the blankets. "That fireplace never worked well." The woman's voice was as toneless as though it came from the bottom of a well.

"It didn't turn itself on," Lois retorted. She wished the words came out clearer, wished her head were clearer. It was desperately important for her to think clearly and she couldn't seem to do it. Her thoughts were tangled as her feet had been in that monstrous nightmare when she had fled in panic from Clyde who had pounded after her, with Paula screaming for help from a man who could not answer because he was dead.

Bessie straightened up without looking at her. "Why don't you go back to New York, Mrs. Fleming? This cottage isn't healthy."

Lois found herself laughing hysterically and used all her will power to check the wild sounds that came tearing from her throat.

"Want me to stay?" Bessie asked when the paroxysm was over.

"No," Lois said quickly. She added, "Thank you."

She locked the door after Bessie, staggering like a seasick passenger on a pitching deck, started to close the windows and then with a shudder decided that it was safer to leave them open.

I won't go to sleep, she decided. I'll stay awake in case — whoever it was — comes back. I wish I had a gun.

Someone tapped quietly on the Dutch door. Tapped again. Softly. A ghost of a sound. She did not move although she knew she must be visible in the lighted room. She could not move.

And then Shandy spoke at one of the open windows. "Lois," he said in a low tone, "turn out the lights and let me in."

ii

And after a pause that seemed interminable, she did. She snapped off the switch, released the bolt on the Dutch door and then moved back, retreating step by step in the darkness.

Shandy found her with groping hands and drew her into his arms. They hardened around her as he pressed his cheek against hers. At last he released her and settled her on the couch, a blanket tucked around her neck.

"Cold in here," he said.

"I had to leave the windows open because of the gas." Her words still sounded muddled.

His hand reached for hers, found it. "I've been almost out of my mind."

"Carol says I'm out of my mind," Lois told him. "And Dr. Thomas wants to make me believe I turned on the gas myself. I told him —"

"What did you tell him?" Shandy sounded as though he had been running. After a moment he repeated, more evenly, "What did you tell him?"

"I told him someone was trying to kill me the way Roger had been killed." And this time the words were distinct. She freed her hand.

At last Shandy said soberly, "Well, the fat is in the fire now. We'd better be prepared for trouble."

Lois laughed shortly. "Be prepared! If attempted murder isn't trouble I'd like to know what is."

"I don't believe it was an attempt to kill you."

How little you can make of a voice alone, Lois thought. Without a key to Shandy's expression, it was impossible to guess what he was really thinking.

"What do you believe it was?" she asked drily.

"A warning. After all, Ethel found you before any real harm had been done."

Ethel. Lois thought about the pockmarked secretary. "No, it couldn't be Ethel. She would never have killed Roger. She loved him. Just what did happen, do you know? Ethel said you were here."

Ethel had gone racing up to his cottage when she found the room full of gas. She had left the door open but she was afraid to go inside to open the windows and turn off the gas jet. He had done that and applied first aid while she got help. Bessie had come and then Carol and, after what seemed like an endless time, Dr. Thomas. He had been delayed by a flat tire.

"Then it was you who saved my life," Lois said. "Shandy, who did it?"

He was silent.

"It's no good trying to cover up any more, you know," she said again. "I have no intention of being a sitting duck for a killer. Tomorrow I am going to call the police. And if Dr. Thomas makes the slightest suggestion, the faintest hint, about my sanity, I'll call every doctor in the country." She sat up abruptly. "Where was Clyde? Bessie came — but not Clyde."

"I don't know," he said without interest. "But it wasn't Clyde."

"How do you know?" When he made no reply she said, "I have a right to be told."

"Yes," he agreed heavily. "You have a right to be told. It was a woman." A dim circle of light gleamed as he lighted a flash after muffling it with his handkerchief. "I found this caught in the gate." The light shone on a tiny scrap of black velvet. "What with its color and the darkness I'd never have seen it if my key hadn't stuck. I had my flashlight on it and this scrap of cloth was caught on that jagged nail beside the lock."

A woman. Carol, Ethel, Bessie, Paula. And

Paula was beyond suspicion because she was in the big house with her leg in a cast. After all, elimination was simple. Neither Bessie nor Ethel dressed in black velvet. Carol had been wearing a pale blue satin housecoat when she came to the cottage but that meant nothing. If she had noticed the tear she had plenty of time to change. And no evidence against her, as there had been no evidence against her when Roger died. Except for a fragment of black velvet in Shandy's possession.

"Shandy," she said, keeping her voice level, "I want that scrap of velvet."

"No. It's safer with me. And you — are safer."

"Do you love her so much?"

Shandy's laugh startled her in the darkness. An ugly sound. So ugly that she wanted to cry out, "Stop it! Stop it!"

Then he got up. "I'll be outside all night. If you want anything, call."

"But —"

"I can sleep all day tomorrow," he said impatiently. The tips of his fingers touched her cheek. "You're safe. Remember that."

She heard his halting steps cross the room. The smoke of a cigarette drifted in through the window and mingled with the odor of gas.

For a long time Lois lay staring at the ceiling. So it was Carol, and Shandy knew. He had known all along. But he wouldn't — surely he wouldn't — let it happen again.

A fresh breeze swept through the room, blowing

out the gas, leaving untainted air behind it. She could not smell Shandy's tobacco now. Perhaps he had fallen asleep on the terrace. The gust of wind died down.

The night was still, so still that the sound of the shot seemed as loud as though it were outside the window.

SIXTEEN

Shandy was fumbling at the Dutch door.

"I'm awake," she called to him. "What is it?"

He was inside the room now. "I don't know. Sounded like a shot down at the big house."

"You'd better go."

"I don't like leaving you."

"I'm all right now. Really."

"Lock your doors then. And don't let anyone in — not anyone — until I get back. I'll come as quickly as I can." He hesitated for a moment and then went out. She heard him running toward the house.

Shandy didn't do it, she thought. Shandy didn't do it. She felt fine. She slid her feet out of bed and dressed quickly. Then she propped chairs under the doors and turned off the switch. The darkness made her uneasy but she was more afraid of the light. Because obviously the gun had been found and someone had fired through the window in the cottage once before. She pushed her chair out of range and settled down to wait.

And remembered that only a few hours earlier someone had entered the cottage and turned on the gas while she slept. She did not ask herself who. She asked why. It was not because she knew who had killed Roger but because she would never rest until she did know. There was no one who had not warned her to let it alone. No one who loved Roger enough to want to find his murderer. And then her breath caught in her throat. Well, she exclaimed, so that's it! But that is impossible.

It was so impossible that she refused to think about it and she had to think or she would begin listening for footsteps outside the window in the dark. Something had happened at the big house but it no longer touched her. Because Shandy was out of it; he had been on her terrace. Shandy — well, for heaven's sake, she thought in amazement. She smiled in secret delight. She forgot to listen for footsteps.

Shandy ran across the lawn to the big house. The hedge rustled as he passed it. Someone is there, he thought, but he did not stop. Because of the screams.

He opened the side door, ran through the library and into the main hallway. The screams were coming from Carol who stood at the top of the stairs, her eyes blank, her mouth opening on those ghastly sounds. He raced up the stairs and gripped her by the shoulders.

"Carol!" He shook her. "Carol."

She looked at him without recognition and the screaming went on. He lifted his hand then and slapped her hard across the cheek. The screams broke off, Carol jerked away from him and said in a high thin voice, "Why did you kill him, Shandy? Why did you kill him?"

There was a gasp from the hallway below and Shandy turned to see the Hatterys looking up at them.

"Who was killed?" he demanded then.

"Doc. It's Doc."

"Where?"

Carol made a gesture, vague and uncoordinated, and he went into Paula's room. The girl lay, waxen white, on her pillows and Doc was sprawled across the foot of the bed. A red stain spread slowly over the white sheet. For one hideous moment Shandy thought they were both dead. Then he shoved Carol unceremoniously to one side, touched Paula's cheek and reached for her wrist.

"She's all right," he said in a tone of relief, "she just fainted."

He bent over Doc who lay as he had fallen, blood oozing from a hole in his thigh. Shandy straightened up. "He's not dead and I don't believe he is seriously hurt. We'll have to get a doctor out here. And the police."

"No," Carol said.

"Don't be absurd, Carol. If we don't call the police ourselves, any doctor we get will do it when he finds Doc Thomas has been shot. He'll have no choice."

The Hatterys had crowded into the room and Ethel unexpectedly took charge. "First," she said, "we'll have to move Doc, get him off that bed."

At her orders, Shandy and Joe lifted the un-

197

conscious man and carried him into a guest room where Shandy, at Ethel's orders, removed Doc's trousers while she brought towels, hot water, and made a tourniquet to stop the bleeding.

And all the time she talked, words pouring out of her as though floodgates had been opened. "What a fool I've been. I thought — I was afraid — it was Joe who'd done all this."

"That's why you smashed the pane of glass."

She nodded. "I thought he was jealous of Roger Brindle and so I was partly to blame for what had happened to Roger. It has been hell, thinking that. But Joe had no reason to harm Mrs. Fleming or Doc. He didn't do it. Thank God, Mr. Stowe, I can leave him now I'm free of him."

The uncharacteristic loquacity stopped. She said in her usual tone, "Get some brandy."

As he started toward the stairs he saw Carol standing as he had left her at the foot of Paula's bed. Joe was crouching, one arm stretched out under the bed.

"Don't touch that gun, Joe!" he said sharply. "Leave it where it is."

Joe grinned. "I just wanted to look at it." He gave a sidewise glance at Shandy. "A .22. That's what I figured."

"Out," Shandy said, and after a moment's hesitation Joe left the room with a last glance at Paula unconscious on the bed and Carol still standing at the foot, her eyes blank.

Ethel held Doc's head and let a little brandy trickle down his throat, careful not to choke him.

He swallowed, opened his eyes, and almost instantly he was alert.

"Good work," he told Ethel, looking at the tourniquet.

"I haven't called a doctor yet," Shandy said. "Who do you want?"

"Bring me my bag," Dr. Thomas replied, "it's in Paula's room. I can deal with this myself."

"You can hardly probe for that bullet."

"I can if I have to," Thomas retorted. "Do as I say. We don't want the police here."

"Who doesn't?" Shandy asked. "Anyhow, this thing has gone too far. Someone is berserk and we'll have to stop it. The truth about Roger is going to come out whether we like it or not."

"Let's not try to pull any wool over each other's eyes," Dr. Thomas said. "I'm in this thing up to my neck. I covered for Carol in the first place and I'm stuck with it now. If that comes out it will just about finish me, especially with people feeling about Roger as they do. But Carol — she got under my skin. I don't know what it is about her." He gave a short laugh. "Now she tries to kill me and I can't do a thing about it. I have to keep still for my own sake."

"Did you see her do it?"

"No, I — well, I —"

"Okay, you were making a few passes. But I'm damned if I can see how you could have failed noticing if she had a revolver in her hand."

"I only — damn it, bring me that bag," Dr. Thomas said harshly and with a shrug Shandy did as he requested.

"Can I help you?" he asked when he had set the bag on the bed within the doctor's reach.

"Ethel will help. And shut the door behind you."

"I'll leave some brandy. Looks as though you are going to earn it." Shandy poured a small amount into a glass and left the bottle for Thomas. In Paula's bedroom he lifted the girl's head and held the glass to her lips. She swallowed convulsively and opened her eyes. They fell on the blood-stained sheet but she did not cry out. Instead she looked at it with a kind of savage delight.

"Carol did it," she said. "She shot Doc. And she killed Roger, too. Dr. Thomas knew. Tonight he told her he knew and he'd protect her if she was nice to him. They thought I was asleep and he was whispering. But he warned her about attacking Mrs. Fleming. He said it had to stop. And he tried to make love to her. Then she shot him."

"Did you actually see her with the gun in her hand?" Shandy asked. "Be careful, Paula. Think before you speak."

His eyes held hers. He watched temptation battle with fear. At length she capitulated sullenly. "No, I didn't see her do it. I was pretending to be asleep because I had to know. But there was no one else here."

"If your eyes were closed, you can't be sure about that."

Malice glinted in her pale eyes. "You want to protect her, don't you? Like Doc. She did it for you, of course. For your money, that is. She needs it."

Paula broke off as sounds came from behind the closed door of the guest room, grunts, curses, a half-stifled sound between a groan and a yelp as Doc probed for the bullet in his thigh.

"I think I'm going to be sick," Paula said.

"Try it," Shandy warned her grimly. "I can take just so much. You pull yourself together."

At length the door opened and Ethel came out into the hall. Shandy went to meet her. She was shaking.

"All right?" he asked.

"He got it out. We did our best — stopped the bleeding and cleaned out the wound as well as we could."

"What about calling another doctor? Suppose there's infection?"

"I don't know," Ethel said wearily. "He said I wasn't to dare call anyone. I don't know. I just wish to God I was out of this madhouse."

High heels clicked on the stairs as Carol came up with a whisper of satin, a wave of perfume. "I telephoned Helen Thomas," she said in a tone of satisfaction. "She was bound to find out anyhow so I thought it was wiser to get her here and make her see reason."

From the guest room Doc shouted furiously, "Carol! You damned fool! Now you've really done it."

When Ethel had run back to the guest room to prevent the irate doctor from getting up, Shandy followed Carol down to the library. She whirled around to face him then, without a trace of her usual languor.

"Shandy," she whispered, "Doc thinks I shot him."

"I gathered that."

"Don't look at me that way! Doc tried to make love to me as though it was a kind of bargain so he wouldn't say anything about what happened to Roger and Mrs. Fleming. As though I'd done it. I think he's crazy."

"But you aren't," Shandy assured her. "Calling Mrs. Thomas — that was really clever of you."

Carol smiled faintly. "She has always been madly jealous of me. Doc won't dare do anything while she is around."

"What could he do?"

"He could cause you trouble," she said flatly. Her manner had changed. "I told him we — expect to marry. And he is in love with me."

"So we expect to marry," Shandy said oddly.

Carol's hand touched his shoulder, her arm crept around his neck. "I've always understood how you felt about me."

"Have you?" He looked down at the face so close to his, poignantly aware of the body that pressed against him. "But do you understand how I feel about Lois Fleming? I warn you, Carol — don't touch her again. Is that clear? I've kept still so far but I won't where she is concerned."

"Shandy!" She sounded bewildered. "Are you trying to blame me — like Doc — like Paula? But I thought you —"

The doorbell rang.

Shandy admitted Mrs. Thomas, who had flung a polo coat over a cotton nightdress and tied a scarf over her hair whose lumps indicated pin curls beneath.

"Where's Doc?" she demanded.

"Upstairs," Shandy said. "He's all right, Mrs. Thomas. I'll take you up."

For a long moment she looked at Carol in the blue satin negligee, then she turned and went up the stairs without a word, moving, Shandy thought, like nemesis.

Unexpectedly Carol ran after her, caught her arm. "Helen, we'll do everything we can to make him comfortable, you know."

The doctor's wife shook off her hand. "You killed Roger," she said deliberately, "so you'd be free to get Doc. I'm not blind. I've watched you for months and I knew as well as you did that you could wrap the poor besotted fool around your finger. But he's my husband. Before I let you have him I'll tell everyone you killed Roger Brindle. I intended to wait, to let Doc come to his senses. Though I did think it my duty to inform Jane Brindle. I wrote to her that there was something mighty queer about Roger's death."

"So that's why she came," Carol cried. "Helen, you left that anonymous letter for me when you and Doc came to take me to the — services."

"I thought it might stop you from thinking you'd got away with it." Mrs. Thomas pushed Carol aside and went up to the room where Ethel stood waiting.

Carol came slowly down the stairs to Shandy. "What happened to Roger?" she demanded. "At first I thought it was suicide. And I couldn't bear to have anyone know. That he hadn't been happy with me, I mean. Of course, I knew it wasn't his heart. The place was full of gas. But when I knew he'd been killed I thought you did it."

"Revenge?" he asked her. "Jealousy? Desire for you? No, Carol. Neither you nor Roger mattered enough."

"Do you like Mrs. Fleming better?"

"I like her better. Carol, do you have a black velvet dress?"

She blinked in astonishment. "What on earth are you talking about?"

"Have you?"

"I had a black velvet negligee. Shandy, you're crazy. What on earth —"

"When did you wear it last?"

"I have no idea. Months ago, I suppose."

"What did you do with it?"

"It was getting shabby so I gave it to Bessie Kibbee. There was so much material I thought

204

she could turn it into a dress or something." Carol looked at him, her mouth partly open. At last she said, "You didn't kill Roger. You didn't — like me enough." When he made no reply she went on, groping her way. "But someone killed him and tried to kill Mrs. Fleming and shot Doc tonight. And the Thomases both think I did it. Only I didn't, Shandy."

Her eyes seemed to grow bigger while he looked at them, bigger, almost sightless. And fear was growing in her face. Her mouth trembled, tears welled up in her eyes and rolled down her cheeks. She really cried beautifully, Shandy thought with detachment. "I don't know what to do," she said, her voice shaking. "Roger always told me what to do."

"But where is Bessie?" Shandy said suddenly. "The Kibbees must have heard that shot. Where are they?"

And he was afraid for Lois, alone in Roger's cottage. He left Carol and ran out into the darkness.

SEVENTEEN

After the brilliantly lighted house the garden seemed very dark. In spite of his driving sense of haste, Shandy waited for a moment to let his eyes adjust to the night. And while he stood still he was aware of cautious movement. Sound is deceptive in the dark and he held his breath to help him listen, trying to determine the direction.

The furtive noises seemed to come both from his left and his right. There were two people sheltered by the dark. Leaves rustled as though someone had brushed against the low branch of a tree. Shandy turned his head to the right, still as a stone. And then, on his left, someone moved. The intruder was unexpectedly, startlingly close, so close that Shandy heard clearly a sharp, gasping breath. A stone grated, rolled under a heel.

Step by step they advanced. The intruder would move a few feet and Shandy would follow. Forward and backward, side to side, they shuffled, along the paths, across the lawn, through the hedges. There was a curiously leisurely pace to this phantom pursuit. As though the thing Shandy followed had no objective at all, as though it moved just ahead of him as aimlessly as some disembodied ignis fatuus.

For what appeared to be endless time he played

a kind of ghostly hide and seek in the dark garden, stalking through bushes that clung like fingers to his clothes and raked his face like nails. What was the fellow trying to do? They were both motionless now, trying to find each other's location. And a branch snapped.

Shandy moved then and the other began to run. It was easy to follow the running footsteps along a path, the steps of someone who was as familiar with the grounds as he himself, who could follow the paths as easily in the dark. While he ran, Shandy wondered who was ahead of him. Not Carol, thank God. That nightmare was over, the fear that she had killed Roger in order to marry him and his money. Not Joe Hattery, whom he had left behind in the big house. Not Doc about whom he had become increasingly curious.

Shandy was hampered by the leg injured in the war. Although no longer perceptibly lame, he could not run for any distance. He would have to get his man before the leg gave out. Man? But it had to be a man, in spite of the scrap of black velvet. The only woman unaccounted for was Bessie. And that was ridiculous.

He put on a burst of speed, his fingers brushed a sleeve and then the intruder swerved, doubling back toward the big house, and at that moment Shandy knew who it was. No one else loomed so big. It was Clyde Kibbee whom he was chasing.

Shandy could feel the familiar constriction in his muscles which meant he could not run much farther. He stood still, heard the thud of running feet as Clyde attempted to circle around him, dived forward in a tackle and brought the other down in a heavy crash. The side of his open hand moved in a sharp chopping motion and Clyde lay still.

Shandy dragged the unconscious man along the path. There was no question of lifting him as his knee had developed a tendency to collapse under him. He abandoned his intention of taking Clyde to his own cottage. He would never be able to drag the big fellow that far.

Lois's cottage was nearest and as he approached he called so as not to frighten her. She flung open the door, her eyes widened and then she stood back and let him haul Clyde into the room.

"Got anything to tie him with?"

"Shandy! You've made a mistake!"

"Hurry," he panted. "You can argue later."

She ran to bring a ball of heavy twine from a drawer in Roger's work table and Shandy tied Clyde's wrists together behind him, tied his ankles, then bent over him as he sprawled on the floor, a giant of a man.

"Is he badly hurt?" Lois asked.

"He'll come around in a few minutes. Scratched up a bit because I had to drag him. Otherwise he's all right." Quickly he told her what had happened at the house, about the attack on Dr. Thomas and the pursuit through the garden. "Sorry I had to bring him here but it won't be for long. I'll call the police."

Because Lois was silent he turned to her. She

was looking down at Clyde's face, young and defenseless, now that he was unconscious, oddly vulnerable.

"He looks so — lonely," she said. Shandy laughed shortly and reached for the telephone. "Wait! Don't call the police."

"We can't stand guard over the guy indefinitely," he pointed out.

Lois was absorbed in her own thoughts. "Call Jane Brindle."

"At this time of night? Why?"

Lois was still looking at Clyde. "Because she knows."

"Knows what?"

"What is going on here. Why it is going on. And she has been worried about Clyde."

"Someone ought to be," Shandy said grimly. "Roger killed, you nearly killed, Dr. Thomas shot —"

"No," Lois said. "Not Clyde. He —"

"He hated Roger," Shandy told her. "He blamed him because he had no home life and because he thought Roger stole his girl and because Albert Kibbee carried his hero worship so far he couldn't see his own son. And he was in the garden tonight after that attack on Doc."

"Can't you see he had no reason to harm Dr. Thomas? And he'd never have done anything to frighten Paula. He's been a decoy, Shandy. No, please let me call Jane."

Shandy capitulated. And Lois was right. There had been two people in the garden.

Lois called the inn. The phone rang for a long time before the sleepy manager answered. There was a longer wait while she went in search of Jane Brindle. And at last the lovely, rounded voice.

"This is Jane Brindle speaking."

Lois told her what had happened. "Shandy," she concluded, "wanted to call the police but I thought you —"

"Thank you," Jane said simply. "I'll get there as fast as I possibly can."

When Lois had put down the phone she turned to find Shandy looking at her. Chemistry in the blood? Illusion? Midsummer madness? What did it matter so long as this dark-haired man with the narrow distinguished face blotted out everything else for her?

"Come here," he said and she walked quite naturally into the circle of his arms. But not to refuge. Not to peace. To a passion that was starved, demanding, that caught her up in its turmoil. As though an interrupted moment on a crumbling tower seven years before had come to its inevitable climax without an interval.

"Stop, Shandy, stop!" she said, shaken by the intensity of his need.

"Sorry," he said, his breath coming in gasps. He released her. "But you won't — leave me again?"

She shook her head and a look of peace settled over his face. He reached for her again and then, with a faint smile, dropped his arms.

"Better not," he agreed. "But soon, Lois? When will you marry me?"

"Whenever you like," she said recklessly.

He shook his head in a kind of wonder. "And to think I was afraid to have you come! When Carol told me —" he broke off awkwardly.

"You thought she had killed Roger," Lois said. "You have been trying to protect her."

"You've got to understand about Carol. Of course, you know she was the girl I was engaged to at the time I met you. She's — a lovely creature but she — that's all she has, that lovely face and body."

"That," Lois said in amusement, "is enough."

"Almost enough," Shandy admitted so guiltily that she laughed. "But almost isn't — I always knew that, but it didn't seem to matter. Not until I met you. When your husband died so magnificently to keep his faith I couldn't speak to you then. And I was still engaged to Carol. When I came back, of course, she took one look and didn't want any part of me." He grinned as he saw Lois's expression, and then sobered.

It was not, he told her, Carol's fault. She was what she was. The blame had been his; he had withdrawn into his shell, gone into hiding, tried to pull the hole in on top of him.

"That's why I kept the cottage. Not because of the propinquity but because when I was a kid it was what — oh, what caves are to other small boys. The place where I could go and be alone. Safe. It took you to make me see I didn't

211

need a cave any longer."

When Roger died, he went on, he found himself in a quandary. He had known at once, when he entered the cottage, how Roger had died. The place was still filled with gas. And he knew Roger could not have turned it on.

"Before I could say anything, Doc had Roger's body moved up to the house and announced in ringing tones that his heart had failed. Well," he added in self-defense, "what would you have done? Stirred up the animals? I figured he was covering for Carol — which, of course, was exactly what he was doing. He was infatuated with her and he intended to cash in on his knowledge sooner or later. So I was in one hell of a spot. Because Carol —" he did not finish the sentence. It was unnecessary. Carol had decided to marry Shandy.

"What threw me off," he went on, "was that she went all cryptic. What I took for a confession was actually an attempt to cover up what she believed to be a suicide. And she could not accept that. It was a reflection on her. But meantime Joe Hattery had tried a spot of blackmail on me. And Helen Thomas in a jealous frenzy had left an anonymous letter for Carol. Well, I didn't know how responsible I was. And that's when I heard that you were coming back into my life, when my hands were tied."

Imperceptibly, the windows had grown light, the trees emerged first as shadows and then took on detailed form. The sky was streaked with rose

212

birds began to cheep and then to lift their voices in song. And then the sky was blue, without a cloud, and color came back to the world, many shaded green and the riot that was a wild sweetpea vine. Shandy flung open the door to the terrace and let in the morning.

Clyde opened his eyes, tried to move his hands, and remembered what had happened. Shandy had turned, alert for trouble, when his prisoner stirred. But Lois looked down at the boy and told him swiftly, "Jane is coming. I sent for Jane Brindle." The sound of her voice was like a hand held out in the dark. Clyde searched her face eagerly and then the light went out of his small eyes.

"You shouldn't have done that," he said flatly. "You'd better call the police and get it over with."

In the country quiet they heard the distant slam of a car door and after a few minutes Jane came up the path and into the cottage. Her big mouth worked convulsively as she saw the young giant trussed up ignominiously like a fowl.

And behind her Bessie Kibbee exclaimed, "What are you doing to Clyde?"

"What have you done to him, Bessie?" Jane asked gravely. "Hidden him, concealed him, starved him of love in order to maintain an illusion and to protect yourself. Taught him to hate Roger, to believe it was because of Roger he couldn't come here. Cheated him of the devotion, the understanding that was his birthright."

She turned to Clyde. "Whatever has happened,

I am partly to blame. I should never have let you be victimized from the day I found out, a month ago. You should have been told the truth. You were kept away by Bessie because you have grown more and more to look like your father. You are Roger's son."

In the doorway Bessie cried savagely, "I'll kill you for this, Jane!"

"No," Jane said sorrowfully. "No, Bessie. There has been enough killing."

ii

"Clyde didn't kill — his father." Bessie spoke with lips as stiff as though they had been numbed by novocain. "He didn't hurt anyone. He couldn't hurt anyone."

"You know he didn't," Jane agreed readily. "I think your boy discovered who has caused all this horror and he has been acting as a red herring. Clyde has a rare quality — loyalty."

Bessie's fingers fluttered aimlessly around her lips. Her skin was as gray as wet clay. "I didn't want to hurt you, Clyde. But I guess it took me a long time to love you as I should. Because Albert came first. He needed me. I couldn't let him be hurt. You can see that." She waited for a word of reassurance but no one spoke. Clyde sought for something in her face, failed to find anything but remorse, looked away.

"It was bad enough," Bessie went on, "to have

Albert creating Roger in his own image, making a saint of him. I used to try to stop it but after awhile I realized I couldn't take that away from him. He'd built his whole life on a dream. If he couldn't believe in Roger any more he wouldn't have anything. Roger was Albert's career, his ambition, his ideals. Everything he had. All he had. Only I hoped, when Roger was dead, perhaps he'd turn to you."

"What have you done," Shandy asked her, "with the black velvet negligee that Carol gave you?"

"I —" Bessie gasped, whirled and ran out of the cottage with the cumbersome, awkward movements of the middle-aged.

"So that's why Paula called me Roger," Clyde said, dazed by the revelation, but applying his new knowledge first to his obsessive love. "Because I look enough like him so that she noticed it when she was drugged."

"Your eyes and your coloring are Bessie," Jane said, "but your size, your features are a lot like Roger's. That's why Bessie kept you away after you grew up. There isn't a startling resemblance and your expression and personality are completely different. Still, if a person had any reason to suspect the relationship there'd be little doubt. And Clyde — Roger never knew you existed, that is, he never knew you were his son until you came back from the army. When you were younger you looked so much more like your mother. I saw Roger in New York a month ago and he told me then. He was heartsick. He always wanted children. If he had only known before —"

"Did he desert my mother?" Clyde asked.

"It wasn't like that," Jane said. "It was — one of those things. Roger was always attractive to women and Bessie — she wasn't a pretty girl; no one noticed her. And she — made the advances." As he started to speak she went on quickly, "These aren't nice things to say but it's long past time to have a little fresh air and truth on this situation. Bessie found out that Roger was sorry for her and she hated him for that. Poor Roger! His compassion brought him so much unhappiness and created so much for others. But Bessie never told him about the baby. And she wanted desperately to conceal from Albert the fact that the boy was not his own. Roger had introduced them and Albert married Bessie right after she broke with Roger. He never knew Clyde was not his own boy."

Shandy bent over, cutting the cord that tied the boy's hands. "What were you up to out there in the garden?" he asked curiously. And then answered his own question. "Oh, of course, you were trying to keep me from catching Bessie."

Lois started to speak, checked herself and met Jane's eyes.

Clyde tugged at the cords on his ankles. "Cut them," he said. "Let me get up."

"No," Lois cried warningly. "No, don't let him go yet. Follow Bessie. Hurry, Shandy, hurry!"

He pounded across the lawn to the Kibbee cottage. The door was wide open. The living room was empty. In the bedroom Bessie was saying, "Albert, I have to do it. But I love you."

After a horrified glance, Shandy hurled himself across the room. Bessie, tears pouring down her cheeks, was holding a pillow on top of Albert's face. And over his light pajamas Albert wore a black velvet housecoat.

EIGHTEEN

Congratulations," Mignonne said over the telephone. "It's a superb job. One of your best. Roger Brindle's readers will love it and one of the major book clubs has been asking for it. Partly because of the publicity, of course. Anyhow, I'm getting you a cut on the book club. And I have a wonderful assignment for you."

"No," Lois said quickly. "No more jobs. I'm going to be married."

"But this one —"

"There's someone at the door." Lois put down the telephone and admitted an elderly messenger with a long box of flowers bearing Shandy's card and a phrase in his writing that brought color into her face.

Jane Brindle, sitting at a window of Lois's Murray Hill apartment, smiled. "Love agrees with you. And with Shandy. I've never seen such a change in a man. I'm so happy for you both."

Lois stepped over suitcases, tissue paper, and boxes in the cluttered room to find vases. While she arranged the flowers she said soberly, "And yet this happiness has grown out of Roger's death. It —"

"Don't think of it that way. To know that, even indirectly, he had a part in such happiness

— Roger was really good, Lois. Mistaken, yes. But good in a way Albert could never have understood. Warmly, humanly good. Compassionate. While Albert —"

Lois set the vases of fragrant deep red roses on the table. "Jane, did you know from the beginning that it was Albert Kibbee who had killed Roger?"

"I guessed from the moment I got Helen Thomas's anonymous letter. Helen, of course, thought Carol had done it to be free to marry Doc. But I was afraid because, just a month earlier, I had seen Roger in New York. He told me then about Clyde. The boy had been home only a week but by that time Roger was convinced he was his son. There were so many points of resemblance. Roger was heartsick, not only because he had wanted children but because he had neglected his boy. And then he could not help worrying for fear Albert would see what he had seen."

"But to kill him for a thing done more than twenty years before!"

"It was more complicated than that." Jane leaned back in her chair, her hands clasped lightly on her lap, with that indefinable air of serenity about her that brought rest to the people with whom she was. "Albert broke up our marriage. I have wondered ever since if I could have prevented it but the thing was so insidious."

Albert, she explained, had been a little man with a big dream. A dream of perfection. He had set his heart on the ministry and he had failed not once, but over and over. His voice, his appearance, an inexorable vein of iron that made him as ruthless with his parishioners as with himself defeated his purpose.

"What he wanted," Jane explained, "was to worship God perfectly. He is partly a mystic, partly a child, with enormous potentialities for good. So long as he believed in good, that is. But a child — there is nothing so cruel, Lois, nothing so hard of heart as a child."

In time, Albert came to the conclusion, that, in himself, he could not accomplish his purpose of leading men to perfection. But there was Roger; Roger whose personality attracted where his repelled; who warmed where he chilled; who, less intelligent than Albert, had always been far more influenced by him than he realized. So Roger became the instrument through whom Albert worked. And Roger, warped by childhood loneliness and emotional insecurity, had tried to be the man Albert expected him to be.

"I was incredibly blind," Jane said. "It was years before I realized fully what was happening to Roger and by then I could not do anything. If I had tried to make him see that he had become unreal, a puppet of Albert's, I'd only have destroyed him. Because he had to be believed in and I couldn't believe in him any more. I tried and tried but, because we loved each other so much, he knew. And at last the only way I could help him was to get out of his life."

That, Jane added grimly, had been Albert's biggest triumph, for now Roger was his to develop as he chose.

"That's why Albert refused to see me when I came back. He was afraid because we had always been wary of each other, in a way."

"David and Goliath," Lois said suddenly. "The librarian was right. David and Goliath. How did it happen, Jane?"

"Clyde came home and Albert saw the resemblance and knew he was Roger's son. Knew that Roger had sinned and deceived him. Knew that the image he had molded with his own hands to worship was not perfect. And Albert never learned to tolerate imperfection. Just as he had abandoned his churches, so he destroyed the flawed image.

"In a way, Paula precipitated all this. Albert went to see Roger one night and through the window he got a fine view of Paula in the cottage. Evidently the little fool was making quite a nuisance of herself. Albert was profoundly shocked. His idol was making love to his wife's niece. Decadence. Immorality. Sin. He went for Shandy's revolver and shot through the window. A kind of symbol of a thunderbolt from God. A divine warning. But that act of violence, what he regarded as a kind of divine authority, released something in him. Two nights later he went to talk to Roger, to reason with him, and found him dead drunk. Another sin. And that is when he smashed the image. He turned on the gas and

221

when he knew Roger was dead he collapsed.

"Bessie put him to bed and took away his clothes. But by that time Albert was re-creating his perfect Roger again. A Roger who could never fall short of his dreams. It seemed to him quite natural for Doc and Carol to conceal the — execution, I suppose it appeared to him. Nothing must diminish Roger's reputation. And then you came unexpectedly, before the cottage had been touched. You wondered. And Albert was wild because Bessie kept him *hors de combat*. So he locked his door to keep her from discovering he wasn't there and he went prowling at night, wearing that black velvet housecoat to hide his light pajamas. It wasn't until Doc said Roger had killed himself that Bessie guessed the truth. Until then she had believed in the heart attack. At first she was afraid Clyde had killed Roger out of jealousy. Then at the last she saw, as Clyde saw, and they both tried to protect him."

"But why shoot Dr. Thomas?"

"Because Roger's wife must be faithful to his memory."

"And why — me?" Lois asked.

"Because you wouldn't let go. You were determined to find out the truth. And you have a kind of awareness about people. Sooner or later you would know. As you did know."

Lois nodded. "But I didn't believe it, if that makes sense. What will they do to him?"

"I don't know. There's not much concrete evidence. No fingerprints on the gun or on the gas jet. Only a torn scrap of black velvet caught on the gate and the housecoat Albert was wearing with the tear in it. That's not actually much of a case. Because Doc won't talk about Roger's death; he'll never change his evidence. He won't accuse Albert of shooting him. In the first place, he'd have to tell why. And anyhow he didn't actually see Albert with the gun in his hand. No one did. Albert stood in the dark hallway in that black velvet robe. He was practically invisible."

"But where did he get the gun?"

"He buried it on the terrace after shooting through the window. Paula found it and left it in the house. Bessie took it to her cottage to keep anyone else from being hurt. There Albert found it again.

"Poor Bessie! They won't let her see Albert, you know. She tried to smother him to save him from a trial and they are afraid she'll find a way to smuggle poison to him. She sacrificed her son to him and now she has lost them both. I've got Clyde a job in New York and he's going to live at my apartment until he finds a place of his own."

Lois closed a suitcase, locked it and straightened up. As she looked around the cluttered room she grimaced. "Of all the demoralizing experiences, moving is the worst."

"Where are you and Shandy going to live?"

"Carol is selling the house back to Shandy for an outrageous price, going on to greener pastures, and we'll live there when we get back from South America."

"Your Shandy," Jane remarked, "caused me some bad moments. The day you came to see me at the inn, Joe Hattery had just left. He knew I was fond of Shandy and he intimated I'd better persuade him to play ball. I sent for Shandy and we talked it over."

"So that's where he was when Paula was lost! You know, Jane, the Hatterys —"

"I know," Jane agreed. "Ethel Hattery is the worst danger Albert has to face. She hates him for killing Roger. If he goes to the chair it will be largely her doing."

The telephone rang and Lois answered it eagerly, hoping it would be Shandy. Over the telephone Mignonne said firmly, "Lois, about that new assignment. Murray Gilbert, the book collector, wants you to do a story on his collection. You'll love it."

"No," Lois said. "No."

"He'll pay two hundred a week."

"But why? That sort of job's not worth it."

The house buzzer rang and Jane, in answer to Lois's wave, pressed the bell.

"Someone in his family has been feeding him arsenic."

"I won't. I simply won't get involved."

Mignonne played her trump card. "This time there won't be an 'as told to' angle. You'll sign your own name."

Someone ran up the steps, tapped at the door.

"Oh." Lois wavered. "Well, in that case —"

The door opened and Shandy came in. "Sorry," Lois said. "I have another assignment."

We hope you have enjoyed this Large Print book. Other G.K. Hall & Co. or Chivers Press Large Print books are available at your library or directly from the publishers. For more information about current and upcoming titles, please call or write, without obligation, to:

G.K. Hall & Co.
P.O. Box 159
Thorndike, Maine 04986
USA
Tel. (800) 223-6121 (U.S. & Canada)
In Maine call collect: (207) 948-2962

OR

Chivers Press Limited
Windsor Bridge Road
Bath BA2 3AX
England
Tel. (0225) 335336

All our Large Print titles are designed for easy reading, and all our books are made to last.